Late for Dinner

By
MK Scott

Books by M K Scott

The Talking Dog Detective Agency
Cozy Mystery
A Bark in the Night
Requiem for a Rescue Dog Queen
Bark Twice for Danger

The Painted Lady Inn Mysteries Series
Culinary Cozy Mystery
Murder Mansion
Drop Dead Handsome
Killer Review
Christmas Calamity
Death Pledges a Sorority
Caribbean Catastrophe
Weddings Can be Murder
The Skeleton Wore Diamonds

The Way Over the Hill Gang Series
Cozy Mystery
Late for Dinner
Late for Bingo (October 2018)

Chapter One

LOLA STARED AT her manicured fingers gripping the card deck with the same disgust she'd shown when she discovered the local television station had replaced her favorite crime program with a teen reality show.

Her elderly bridge partner, Herman, had a shock of silver hair that waved over his skull similar to a rooster's comb. Any hair in a man's later years was all gravy to the point most of the other male residents grumbled that Herman was a show-off.

He waved his hand in front of her face. "Still breathing? Good partners are hard to come by."

"Don't I know it." She shuffled, ignoring the twinge of pain in her hand.

Marcy and Jake laughed at her comment, but Herman narrowed his eyes, probably taking it as an insult regarding his failure to get the last two trumps.

Lola dealt out a card, still out of sorts, but not quite able to put her finger on why and retorted, "Retirement stinks!"

Marcy, always a calmer member of the group, shot her an easy smile that hardly creased her face. Most folks would think she was younger than her forty plus years with her dark hair hardly touched by gray and her trim body. The only old thing about her was the wheelchair, which was temporary.

If Lola had had a clue that chasing criminals would have kept her looking young, she might have chosen that as a career as opposed to making use of her long legs and other notable assets as a Vegas showgirl. Still, it had been a good life. Her ability to sum up people in a few seconds allowed her to have more than her share of pleasant adventures and adoring admirers. That was behind her. She sighed and acknowledged Marcy with a nod, curious to hear what the woman might say.

"Hear ya. Most working folks would envy us. We're all living in a premier assisted living community with plenty of activities. What else could you want?"

Lola pursed her lips and rolled her eyes upward as she tried to explain how she felt without insulting her companions. "Sure, we have shuffleboard, fit and sit exercise class, flower arranging, and Bible Bingo. Those are old people things. Even the food has morphed into tasteless mush."

"About that." Jake held his hand up. "Something is going on with the dietary director." He glanced around making sure he had everyone's attention and cupped his ear with his hand. "I hear things."

A general murmur of agreement followed, with the exception of Gus yelling, "What?" He sat at a nearby table playing solitaire. Gus didn't know how to play bridge and had no desire to learn.

Various eyes connected around the table, knowing the inevitable process of repeating what had been said in a much louder decibel would probably result. Gus's early life of working with explosives damaged the man's hearing. Even though he had hearing aids, he usually didn't wear them, because he thought they made him look old.

Instead of yelling his former comment, Jake ran a hand over his shoe polish black hair before mouthing the words. Gus popped up both thumbs, signaling his understanding. At some point, he taught himself to lip read, but it only worked if he was directly looking at a person.

Jake had dropped his hand, but put it up again to brandish one finger. "I just happened to overhear the director's phone call." His face crinkled into an impish expression, as if overhearing a conversation in a private office was an everyday thing. Most knew that Jake had served as a scout in the army, but his ability to locate certain information made Lola suspect he might have done even more.

Herman chuckled, but Marcy gestured for Jake to continue, which he did with a waggle of his equally dark eyebrows. The man must dye his hair. Not a good quality dye, since it was just a solid black with no variations to give the hair a feeling of depth—obviously not a professional job, either.

Jake waited for silence before proceeding. "The new gal bragged to an unknown person on the other end that she has absolute control of the food purchase."

"Makes sense," Herman grunted his retort. "What's the big deal?"

"Oh, there's more, much more." The corners of his lips tugged upward. "She went on to brag about how she is gradually changing the menu and still submitting old invoices with doctored dates. It's easy enough to do with a scanner and Photoshop."

"That explains the dog food we've been getting lately." Lola shook her head.

"Covering it with a nasty sauce or calling it stew doesn't make it any better." Herman cleared his throat as if the thought of the food got stuck in his craw. "The food could be better. What about Karaoke on Sunday afternoons?"

Karaoke was a new event the young activities director thought would enliven the group.

"Ah, come on, that's just pathetic. No one can sing. It's never any fun unless you're two sheets to the wind, which none of us are because of the rules against alcohol. Even worse, it's in the afternoon so no one will miss their early bedtime."

Marcy gave a sympathetic smile and added, "I remember when life used to be exciting."

Jake laughed. "Are you referring to when criminals took pot shots at you?"

Marcy put down her cards and splayed her hand against her chest. "You're right! I do miss dodging bullets. It made me feel alive."

"Dying tends to do that." Lola looked at her cards, grimaced, then continued talking. "You're too old to go dashing after thugs."

Before her car accident while pursuing a law breaker, Marcy still could walk a beat, but most at her age had been assigned to a desk job. With her injuries, being able to walk again would be a gift. Being a desk jockey pushing papers would be an upgrade from the early retirement the chief was pushing for. Retired when she wasn't even fifty. No plans, no money, and no family, which left her with absolutely nothing. All she had were her newfound friends at the home. Worse, there were a couple of eighty plus women named Marcy, too, that really made her feel old. They were the fun senior citizens who occasionally sported funny hats and neon nail polish, more like the adventurous spirits featured on the cruise commercials. Really? How exciting could they be if they were here?

"I have an idea. Something that could be fun. Are you in?" Marcy grinned, possibly aware her friends couldn't resist the unknown when wrapped in such a tempting package.

Jake placed his cards on the table. "It's about time we shake things up around here. Although I wouldn't mind doing something about the food in the process."

Herman shot the man an annoyed look. Even though they were friends, it was obvious Jake irritated Herman. It could be because of Jake's extravagant tales of travel to exotic locales and the beautiful women he met there. It sounded made up, as if the man were trying to convince them he was an international spy, while he never mentioned what he'd done after the war, which was odd.

Lola managed to work details of being a former Vegas showgirl into every conversation. Never mind her run on the stage lasted a few years as opposed to decades. Her collection of glittery tops and dangling earrings reminded folks even when she didn't talk about it.

Age had saddled her with a walker, but it didn't mean she would let herself go. She went to the onsite salon to have her hair done and her nails manicured once a week. Lola sported a square cut topaz ring a gambler had presented her with one night. It hadn't meant anything except that the gambler was flushed with winning. It cost a little to have it resized, but she could still honestly claim it was a gift and that she had been someone's good luck charm.

"Ah, I don't know." Herman grimaced. "You aren't going after my jewel thief's diamonds. I knew I should never have mentioned it to you."

"Herman," Marcy took an audible breath. "No one believes your story but you. It may have been what caused you to end up here."

"Ha, ha, you're so funny, I forgot to laugh." The offended man crossed his arms and glared at them. "I checked *myself* in."

Marcy chuckled at his disgruntled expression, which caused his bushy eyebrows to meet in a V.

"I hope you're not going to come up with something scandalous like last time." Lola used the cards to fan her flushed face. "I was sure we'd get caught."

"Please," Marcy's eyes twinkled as she spoke, "We didn't get caught last time because no one expected residents to break into the kitchen and steal extra cheesecake."

"I doubt they even have cheesecake in the fridge anymore," Jake remarked, then nodded to Marcy. "Sorry, Marcy. Go on."

"Remember, people see what they expect to see. As senior citizens," she paused to grimace, "and at the grand age of fifty, I'm in that group, too. Got my AARP letter the other day. Anyhow, we'll be working on cold cases. We'll be crime solvers."

Herman sat up a little straighter and grinned. "I'm great at solving crimes. I was indispensable to the Legacy Police. I may have helped solve a half-dozen murders."

Jake lifted an eyebrow and gave a dismissive sniff. "So indispensable they let you leave?"

Lola cleared her throat. "Boys, stop it. Marcy is offering us an opportunity, other than waiting around for the therapy dog lady to show up. We can pet her collection of poodles attired in colorful tutus. Personally, I feel sorry for the creatures. No reason for you two to ruin everything with your bickering."

Marcy held her hand up for attention. "I'll need all of you. Every one of you has different life experiences and insights. People say it takes a village to raise a child. Sometimes, it takes a village to solve a crime. Not an entire one because that would muddy things up, but in this scenario, the older the brain, the better."

Jake, Lola, and Herman exchanged confused glances. No one in Western society considered the elderly possessing anything to contribute, judging by commercials aimed at the fifty and over set. Prescription drugs, hemorrhoid cream, and knee replacement surgery made it seem like the only thing anyone wanted from them was their money.

Herman was the first to verbalize what they were all probably thinking. "What do you mean?"

Her upraised hand shifted into a single index finger as Marcy folded down the other fingers. "You guys are familiar with the area. Street names have changed over the years, along with businesses, and the local scandals have been forgotten."

Nothing made sense, but the idea of being needed for something appealed. "Why does this matter?" Lola asked.

Marcy dropped her hand and gave each one of them a thorough stare. "You do realize cold cases happened in the past. Sometimes, as much as a hundred years ago. I only asked for the ones thirty years or later. The current crop of officers on the New Albany force don't have the manpower to solve the cold crimes. After a while, the case is shelved to make way for newer ones. There's always plenty, especially with the wave of strangers that pass through our city during the leadup to the Kentucky Derby. The victims and their families on the old ones deserve closure."

"Well," Herman began, then cleared his throat. "I may be here now, but I'm no native. I spent most of my life in North Carolina, except for my stint overseas courtesy of Uncle Sam. Sure, I'd like to help." He gave a slow wag of his head with his expression despondent. "My buddies Jake and Gus would be more help than I would be. Gus was an explosives expert in the war. He could defuse bombs. I'm sure he'd be good at getting past security or even opening safes."

Jake snorted and slapped the table. "That old codger!"

The man's attitude irritated Lola. She cut him a look that should have sliced him in half if he had bothered to acknowledge it. "As I recall, you didn't successfully sneak away when you four took off for North Carolina."

"I had no clue they weren't supposed to leave." Herman looked pained but still continued speaking. "I would have been more covert about it if I'd known. I blame the fact we were caught because of Eunice Ledbetter. If she hadn't left that note about being kidnapped, no one would have noticed our absence. We're all mobile and able to get around, which results in none of the staff watching us too much."

Lola reached across the table to pat his hand. "You mean they didn't watch *you*. Now, they do. I'm surprised they let you keep your car, but since you're a voluntary admission, I doubt legally they can take it from you. Still, it's good you have wheels. We may need them."

She nodded in Jake's direction. "It's also good that Jake has someone on the inside."

The man lifted his head with both pride and a touch of arrogance. "My niece, Katie, works in accounting. She'll be able to give us the low down on what's happening around the center."

Marcy cut her eyes to him. "You're making it sound like we'll sneak out to solve crimes. I meant we'd meet, go over cases together and do some research on the Internet."

Several sighs of disappointment erupted around the table.

"Okay." Marcy held her hand up again. "When we solve a case, we could go out for a celebratory lunch. I need to stay here. My wheelchair is an issue."

There was a rush of assurances, but Lola's voice cut through them all. "Honey, if I go, you go. Anywhere I can go with my walker, you can go with your chair."

Marcy grinned at the four. "It's settled. All we need is a name for our crime solving group."

There were several suggestions including the words *sleuth* and *mystery*, at which Herman rolled his eyes.

Jake leaned across the table in Herman's direction. "It's easy for you to pooh pooh everyone's suggestions, but I don't hear you making any of your own, hotshot."

"All right, I will. I'm a fan of calling a spade a spade. It makes sense for us to be The Way Over the Hill Gang."

A heavy sigh escaped Lola, then she sighed again. Her face puckered as if sucking a lemon. Finally, after her initial theatrics, she replied. "That's the unvarnished truth. As much as I might not like it, it suits us just fine."

Chapter Two

T HE NEXT DAY the four of them, plus Gus, met in the empty craft room. There were several projects scattered about the room including hooked rugs, a loom, and a table with a few slices of wood with indecipherable words on them. The one thing they all had in common was that none of them were finished. Most had been abandoned.

Herman's gaze roamed over the various items with disgust. If anyone bothered to ask him, he would have told them if he hadn't had any interest in something in his previous eighty years, he wasn't picking it up now.

Gus bounded into the room and twirled around as if he were eight instead of seventy-eight. "Woo wee! Let's get this party started."

Great. Good chance his friend would be like that all day. Although he'd never admit it aloud, Herman wondered if some of those close calls with explosive ordinance hadn't rattled something loose. The medical staff might slap a label on Gus like dementia, but it wasn't a full-time thing. Most of the time, he could be as lucid as anyone. Other times, he could be almost giddy.

Herman's eyes rolled upward as he tried to recall their war days together. Ah yes, back when he could see forever and his hair was full and dark. The three of them formed a tight bond during boot camp, realizing they might be going to their deaths in a matter of weeks. Jake and he trained as infantrymen, while Gus was picked for explosives training. It puzzled him that they'd pick his light-hearted friend for disassembling bombs, but he assumed those who chose knew what they were doing. Then again, Gus could have volunteered. That would be such a Gus maneuver. He never admitted to doing so, insisting he had a very special set of skills, proven by the fact he hadn't been blown up, yet.

It might have been skill, but Herman felt the man had more than his share of luck. He probably had a platoon of guardian angels, especially considering the explosive experts went ahead of the troops with a padded vest, a helmet, and a long pole searching for trip lines. It was considered a step up from the previous method, which involved using hands. Whenever Gus warmed up to the subject, he claimed today's soldiers were a bunch of pansies, operating robots from a safe distance to deal with possible bombs.

The squeak of Marcy's chair wheels on the waxed tile floor announced her entrance. "Come on. Gather around and put on your thinking caps. I have a few cases for you. The first one is murder."

Lola feigned a gasp. "Murder! Oh my! This is exactly like my favorite crime drama except the death would have been more recent."

The group moved toward a table with Jake jogging ahead to pull a chair out of the way for Marcy to be able to roll into place. The man never missed a chance to play the gentleman. He canted his head toward Lola. "I bet you imagine yourself as the next Miss Marple."

"Are you kidding?" Lola made a moue of distaste. "I have a degree of sophistication and attitude. Kinda think of myself more like Angie Dickenson in *Police Woman*."

"Angie, huh." Herman placed both thumbs under his suspenders and puffed out his chest. "I might as well be Magnum, P.I. then."

The slap of file folders stopped the good-natured bickering. Marcy opened the first folder and glanced through the notes. Her lips pulled down into a frown and she shuffled the first folder underneath the second.

Herman noticed her actions, even if the others didn't. "What was wrong with that case?"

Marcy opened the second folder, scanned the first page, before looking up at him with a pleased look. Her finger tapped the page. "This was the one I wanted. The other wasn't really solvable."

Gus grabbed a seat and jumped into the conversation. "Isn't that the definition of a cold case?"

"Not really." Marcy pulled the first folder out and waved it. "This one might exemplify it. Drifter turns up dead. No connections to anyone in New Albany. Good chance whoever killed him was a transient. Sometimes, a case goes cold when more pressing cases show up, stretching law enforcement resources."

Outside of Marcy, Herman was the only one who had investigation experience. Yet, he wasn't getting a word in edgewise or demonstrating his expertise. "Isn't it true that if a murder isn't solved within forty-eight hours, the window of opportunity closes?"

"Looks like someone has read up on their criminal investigation. I think that particular statement has shown up on every crime show since the 1950s. Truth is, many cold cases could be solved if there were enough dedicated resources. We, friends, are that resource. Ready to hear about our case?"

There was a chorus of yeses and yays, which made Herman grin. At last, he was doing something that mattered. He was grateful for the change in his daily routine. They may not solve the crime, but he was willing to give it all he had. It was certainly better than watching the country cloggers kick up their heels and make a horrendous amount of teeth grating clatter.

Marcy took a slow look around the room as if looking for listening ears. "All right, investigators. Feel free to take notes."

"Notes." Gus sat up straight in his chair and pushed his slipping glasses up his nose. "No one mentioned anything about notes."

Lola pulled a notebook out of her walker basket and flourished the glittery book. "A good detective is always prepared."

Drat. Herman didn't bring anything. He had no idea Marcy would directly jump into a case. His initial thoughts concerned an organizational type of meeting where they'd elect officers, make rules, decide on dues, and create a secret handshake or door knock.

Lola clicked her pen and hovered it over her open notebook making all the men appear like sluggards.

Marcy nodded and went back to flipping pages. "Okay. Some of you have lived in the area for a while. A few of you moved away and came back. The story might be familiar to you. Twenty-two years ago, Sue Ellen Makowski died. She was the wife of a wealthy businessman and probably as close to a socialite as New Albany had at the time."

"How did she die?" Jake asked the question before Herman could. He closed his eyes briefly, then opened them, not wanting anyone else to get the jump on him.

"Well, the papers declared it was a suicide."

"Pills?" Lola asked, causing Herman to slap the table in frustration.

He had to have his say. "Who said it was suicide?"

"Looks like…" Marcy's finger went down the page. "…the housekeeper, Mabel Elliot, found her." She pointed to Lola. "As for method, she was shot. Point blank in the head."

Herman winced, having a hard time imagining someone resorting to such a dramatic method of leaving this world. A memory of something he heard surfaced. "I always heard women suicides are usually something like drugs or even jumping from a bridge."

"He's right." Lola volunteered. "You say the woman was a socialite. Even if she wasn't a natural beauty, she'd have the money to fix herself up. Comes with the position. I can't believe a woman would kill herself in such a manner. If I ever thought of exiting on my own, I'd fix my hair, put on my makeup, put on my best clothes and jewelry, then I'd choose a method that wouldn't undo all I had just done. Possibly pills. Doesn't sound like a suicide to me."

Herman found himself nodding with Lola's assumption. "Why didn't the police pursue it?"

"There *is* a sticky note on the file. It was placed here after the case was closed. The detective who gave me the case wrote that the detective on this case was his father. His father died last year from cancer, but this was a case that haunted him. Anyhow, the note mentioned the case was closed due to the pressure from Sue Ellen's family. They were tired of seeing their daughter's name on the news and in the papers. They were willing to accept that their daughter committed suicide. The lead detective wasn't satisfied with the suicide conclusion and neither am I."

Chapter Three

MARCY GLANCED AROUND at the residents she'd invited to help her solve her cold case. A thrill lifted the hairs on her arm, while considering she was closer to being back on the force again. Not exactly, but it was certainly better than playing bridge with the senior citizens who weren't above cheating to put a little excitement into their tedious routine. Her age and her shattered leg should earn her a desk position if the current commissioner would allow her to go back. However, he was pushing for an early retirement with a partial disability payout. Most people would take it, then start on the second half of their professional life, but being a police officer was her life. Her dedication to the profession had even put a major knot in her love life. Most people admired a policeman but had issues with a female in the same profession.

Her nose wrinkled as she considered the various men who had passed through her life who were unwilling to understand her job required her response at inconvenient times. Then, there was the inevitable argument about whose job was most important. Obviously, hers was—not that anyone else saw it that way. No, the stockbroker felt his life mattered more due to his inflated salary. Her eyes rolled up as she tried to recall his name. Something that started with a B. It could have been Brent, Brad, or Barry. Before she could recall the correct name, she heard some noises outside the door. They'd reserved the room, but that might not stop someone from hanging around the door. She caught Herman's gaze and cut her chin to the door.

The man stood without saying anything. His silent movements didn't even wake Gus who was snoring loudly. Herman stood at the door, then pulled it open suddenly. A screech sounded as someone stumbled inside the opening and dropped to the floor.

Even though most of the residents of the home were unsteady, the complete fall into the room meant the woman pushing up off the floor had been leaning against the door, possibly eavesdropping. The resident stood, brushed off her clothes and grinned. Even though she looked familiar, Marcy couldn't put a name to her, but Herman could.

"Eunice, don't you ever get tired of snooping?"

Well, that answered the question of if she *had* been snooping. Eunice—the name rang a bell.

Herman folded his arms and glared at the woman who looked pleased with herself. "You weren't invited."

"Yes, I noticed, which I assumed was an oversight on someone's part." Both fists ended up planted on her hips as she landed a venomous look on the assembled group, stopping on Gus.

"You invited that old fool. He's asleep!"

Her strident tone startled Gus, who came awake with a jerk. He blinked a few times trying to orient himself, then looked at Eunice. "Oh, it's you. Should have known. You're like a skin rash, always showing up at an inconvenient time."

"Hardy ha ha." Eunice wrinkled her nose as she spoke the words.

Herman stood behind their unwanted guest, appearing flummoxed.

When Marcy had handpicked the seniors, she hadn't chosen them for their muscles, never thinking she'd need a bouncer. Still, she would have thought any one of them could send one elderly woman on her way, until a snippet of information about Eunice surfaced. Not only had the woman decided to join the boys on their North Carolina road trip, but she had left some odd note supposedly about an alleged kidnapper, demanding wine and chocolate. Everyone knew kidnappers needed a little more than a couple of bottles of chardonnay and chocolate bars.

It looked like no one would confront the determined woman. It would be up to her. "All right everyone. We're done here. Thanks for helping out with the plans for the senior garden plot."

Jake, Lola, and Herman gave her a nod, acknowledging they understood her actions. She expected at least one of them to mention there had been no garden plans, but despite their age, they understood the reference and the need for privacy. Gus still acted slightly dazed, which made her question if he'd blurt out what they were talking about. Thankfully, he followed Lola out as she moved so close to Eunice the woman had to jump back to avoid being bulldozed by the walker.

Marcy bundled up her folders, placed them in her bag, then pivoted her chair. Eunice was still there, proving she was even more tenacious than rumors hinted. Well, she might as well take a page from Lola's book. "Coming through." She angled her chair in Eunice's direction, planning on turning before ever getting there.

Personally, she didn't know the woman and didn't have any feelings about her—good or bad. What she didn't need was every resident at the home gossiping about the cold cases. *The Project,* as she liked to refer to the cold cases, was supposed to convince the commissioner she hadn't outlived her usefulness. So far, she hadn't got anything more than a confirmation from other members that it probably wasn't suicide. That was nothing new.

As she approached Eunice, the woman stepped out of the way and grabbed the handles of her wheelchair. "It's shameful the way they left you to push yourself."

Marcy snorted. No way she'd fall into that one. Maybe everyone had underestimated Eunice. The woman was smart enough to know when to play the sympathy card. There had been enough cases where she'd played the good cop to her partner's bad cop routine to recognize it. "I can push myself."

"Oh, I know you can. Why not allow someone to give your arms a break?"

It was hard to argue with that. Although she'd never admit it, her arms were getting a little tired. Before her accident, she would have claimed she was as fit or fitter than any other woman her age. It was hard to bounce back after the accident, and she soon discovered her arms were never in the kind of shape to push a wheelchair non-stop.

Eunice confidently pushed the chair and took turns as if she knew where she was going, which made Marcy wonder what their end destination was. "Where are we going?"

A chuckle served as an answer as the woman kept pushing. The sound of music snaked out of the main meeting room as Eunice steered her in that direction. "We better hurry or someone else will snag all the prizes."

Not Name That Tune! Even though many residents enjoyed the trivia game, most of the tunes were before Marcy had been born. Then there were the prizes, everything from magnifying glasses for doing crosswords, colorful containers for dentures, and crocheted cozies for tissue boxes. No, thank you. It only made her feel older than she already was. Curiosity about Eunice's motives was the only reason she hadn't already taken control of her wheelchair. Enough was enough.

"Thanks for the push, but I think I'll head back." Her hands wrapped around the inner metal wheel that propelled the chair. Her initial attempt to reverse her chair met with resistance. Eunice still hung onto the back of the chair. "You can let go now."

"If I did, you'd just take off on me, and I wouldn't get to say what I need to say."

It took a twist of her body to halfway face her tormentor. It also pinched a nerve in her lower back. Even though it went against her principles to negotiate with her harasser, she'd hear the woman out. "Let's hear it."

"All right." Eunice gave the chair a sudden push and veered in the direction of a table with an open space. The sound of Doris Day singing "Sentimental Journey" had the seniors bouncing in their chairs waving their hands to be called up.

A few of the residents yelled out title suggestions.

"Doris Day!"

"Those Were the Days!"

"Peggy Lee!"

Eunice plopped down on a nearby chair and gestured to the residents. "Just pitiful. Speaking of pathetic people, why would you pick Gus over me for anything?"

On the surface, Gus didn't look like a good choice, but Herman had assured her he'd be a great bet being a local. Besides, breaking up the three amigos would result in a leak of information. Together, they'd keep their lips sealed, viewing it as a joint mission. Still, she needed to come up with an answer that would satisfy her questioner.

"He needs it more than you. Obviously, he isn't the sharp knife you are. I bet people are asking you to join their group due to you being popular." She peered down at her hands afraid a facial tic might give her away.

Eunice's initial look of surprise gave a way to a smug look. "Yeah, that *is* a problem."

"Sentimental Journey" continued to play in the background as various residents continued to guess.

"Que Sera, Sera!"

"Is That All There Is?"

"Mary Had a Little Lamb!"

Eunice shot to her feet, slapped the table, and yelled, "It's Magic! What is wrong with you people?"

Seriously. No one knew what song it was. In a low voice, she hissed, "Sentimental Journey."

The activity director must have supersonic hearing. Using the microphone, she announced, "We have a winner! Raise your hand, Marcy."

A series of silvered heads turned in her direction. Some even displayed baleful glares. It wasn't like she was trying to win. The director walked over to her table with a shiny shopping bag and placed it on her table. "Lucky you. Thanks for coming. Please don't guess anymore, or I might have a riot on my hands."

The residents did take the game seriously. Marcy held up her hands as if surrendering. "I won't answer another one, even if you beg me."

The sound of "Happy Birthday" started playing in the background. The director nodded her head in acknowledgment. "This may look like a game to you, but this is memory therapy for our dementia and Alzheimer patients."

"Oh." That explained why they couldn't guess a simple song. She pushed the sack toward the director. "Take this. I'm sure one of the residents would like it."

Eunice snagged the bag before she could give it back. Her arms wrapped around it possessively. "Check it out before you give it back. It might be something you want."

Yeah sure, like that would happen. Still, she might bash something that everyone else in the room would love to have. "Here, let me look." She held out her hand for the bag, which was surrendered slowly.

Nestled inside the tissue was a wooden rendition of one of the big head guys from Easter Island. "I think it's a figurine."

"Nope." Eunice plucked out the head and put it on the table. She took off her glasses and balanced them on the big nosed figurine. "It's a glasses holder. Keeps your glasses from getting broken."

"I see that." Now that the item had been identified, it grew on her. "I could use that. I'm always misplacing my readers."

An exaggerated sigh greeted her observation as Eunice removed her glasses and handed big head guy over to her. "It's yours. You won it fair and square." Her lips trembled a little. "It would have brought a little joy in my life. Never mind me."

Guilt usually didn't work on her, but not this time. She shoved the bag at Eunice. "You take it."

"Oh no, I couldn't. It would be wrong." She shook her head hard, resembling a head bobbing doll.

What was with the trembling lips and making her feel as if she just ran over a puppy? "Okay." She placed the bag in her lap, then reversed her chair to leave, earning a grateful smile from the director.

Eunice rushed to get in front of the chair before Marcy could get out the door. "Don't worry about me. Sure, I'm not as popular as you think I am. All I wanted was to be part of your garden planning group, but it's just another clique I can't seem to penetrate."

Not the clique ploy. Her heart felt as if a big hand had squeezed it. Due to her family moving every time her father got a transfer, she knew all too well what it was like to be stuck on the outside. Great, now she'd have to start a garden group to cover her cold case group.

"Sure, you can be in the garden group."

Eunice pressed her hands together. "Really?"

"That's what I said." She'd have to warn the others before Eunice mentioned it. It would mean twice the number of meetings, but it wasn't like she had that much on her schedule.

"You already had one meeting." Eunice released her pressed hand to flourish one finger. "I may have missed a great deal. Maybe you could give me a rundown."

Most people would just be grateful to be in the group. Not Eunice. "Nothing really. We met to come up with a name but couldn't decide on it. Maybe you could take that on as your special project."

"Maybe." Eunice's lips twisted as she considered the possibility. Then she pushed back her shoulders and saluted. "You got it, Captain."

Chapter Four

THE SOUND OF a clear wolf whistle sounded. Herman glanced behind him, eyeing the two elderly ladies who chatted as they strolled past. Neither one of them bothered to give him a second glance, which didn't explain the whistle. Jake had warned him that the women outnumbered the males three to one, claiming as a new guy, the women would line up to meet him. So far, that hadn't happened. Maybe it just took time. His hand rested on his rounded belly, wondering if that was the problem. Instead of having a svelte silhouette, he looked more like Santa Claus minus the beard.

Once the news got out that he'd been the ringleader of the North Carolina jaunt, he had been stamped with the rebel/bad boy image. Women had a hard time resisting the temptation of a bad boy—or in his case, a perceived bad boy—and what it represented. The previous women hadn't even faltered as they sauntered by him. It couldn't be them.

The whistle sounded again. He turned slowly trying to figure out who his mysterious admirer might be. With his luck, it might be Eunice. Wouldn't that be a kick in the pants! Gus and Jake were convinced they were the reason he moved to Greener Pastures Retirement Center. They were in a way, but not the entire reason.

Hanging out at The Painted Lady Inn and watching the slow blossom of the romance between the B and B owner, Donna, and veteran detective, Mark, had made him wistful. Apparently, romance wasn't something reserved for the very young. The only problem with his former residence was the lack of unattached women in the right age category. His friends had implied there were plenty of available women at the center. What they failed to add on was a third wouldn't remember his name the next day. Some younger men might consider that a plus, but he didn't.

Back before Uncle Sam decided he needed his help in the war effort, he had a sweetheart. Instead of next door, she lived a few blocks down. That hadn't worked out the way he planned. By the time he returned, she refused to have anything to do with him. It put him off women. Couldn't trust them. The whistle sounded again.

He shook his head in frustration. It sounded near, but he couldn't see anyone. Who did such a thing? A slender, bearded male in a dark blue shirt that identified him as a maintenance employee grinned in his direction. "Rad ringtone."

"Thanks." He watched the employee disappear down the hall and contemplated the remark. *Ringtone*? He must have meant his phone. Gwen, his great niece, insisted on getting him a cell phone against his wishes. She even set it up for him, adding various bells and whistles he had no interest in having. In this case, actual whistles. She could be calling him right now.

A sense of anticipation surged through him as he inserted his hand into his trouser pocket to find his phone. Gwen was as close to a grandchild as he'd ever had. It tickled him that she chose to call him. Made him feel important. He pulled the phone out his pocket and swiped at the screen until he heard a voice.

"Herman?"

Even though the voice was female, it wasn't his rapscallion niece. He had the phone half up to his ear as the realization hit him, causing his excitement to plummet. Still, a woman called him. When was the last time that happened if he excluded all the fundraising calls? "Hello?"

"It's me, Marcy."

His eyebrows shot up. A younger woman was calling him. Made sense that someone on the young side of sixty would be more familiar with these newfangled phones. His bad boy image must work for all ages. "How can I help you?"

"Eunice."

The name hung in the air between them, shooting darts at his romantic assumption. There was no way Eunice would be ever connected with Cupid, the messenger of love. "What now?"

"I had to tell her we have a gardening club so she wouldn't be sniffing around."

He remembered Marcy's words about a garden club as the meeting broke up with the impromptu appearance of Eunice. The woman referred to herself as an armchair sleuth—another name for *gossip*. "I remember. What's up? Better, why are you calling me?"

Most of the residents avoided the phone declaring it was hard to hear anything, and it would have taken less than ten minutes for him to walk to Marcy's unit.

"I told Eunice she could be in the garden club."

"What?" His hearing must be going, too. He held the phone away from him and regarded it with suspicion. It could be the phone and not him. Sound was still coming out of it though, and he could hear it. He brought it closer to his ear.

"I had to. She was too pitiful, telling me people here didn't ask her to do things with them."

Really? How could a sharp policewoman be taken in by a con artist like Eunice? "There's a reason no one wants to do anything with her. You're relatively new here and probably haven't spent enough time around her to realize her brand of charm—or lack of it—wears on a person."

"Maybe. Still, I told her there was a garden club. We have to have some meetings. I'll have to talk to someone about letting us make some raised plots in the courtyard, too."

Even when the woman wasn't around, Eunice stirred things up. "Getting my hands dirty isn't something I signed up for."

"It probably won't get that far. Anyhow, we have to be very sneaky about our cold case meetings. I need you to contact everyone and get them to my room. Don't come together, that will be obvious. Come one at a time. The meeting will start when everyone has arrived. I made copies of the detective's notes for everyone. See ya."

She hung up before Herman could acknowledge he heard and would follow directions. He stood for a few seconds staring at his phone, then he smiled. He had a mission. Better yet, it was a covert one. Eunice would serve as the enemy he had to get past. His mouth twisted to one side as he considered how he could accomplish his task as quickly as possible.

Bingo! Yes! It was the answer. The rest of the group would be in the Florida room playing Bingo. The prizes were decent, but the room tended to be humid with all the glass panes and the plants crowded into the room to take advantage of the sunlight, which earned it the name of a hot, sweaty state. If he wanted to sweat, he'd have stayed in the South.

He made his way to the room, hoping his sudden arrival wouldn't draw too much attention. Residents in wheelchairs and walkers zoomed past him in an effort to beat him to the game, which was silly. It didn't matter how soon you got there. It didn't make your chances any better. The voice of the caller wafted out of the room along with excited chatter.

"B4."

"Bingo!"

"Again, I swear this game is fixed."

Herman stood in the open doorway and stood transfixed by residents with multiple cards and Bingo dabbers in both hands. The determined set of their mouths and focused stares meant they wouldn't notice him. He should easily be able to extract his crime solving partners. An employee at the door greeted him with a resigned look.

"You're too late. We're out of cards."

That explained the speed of the residents who struggled to get there before him. "It's okay. Just looking for my friends."

The woman gestured to the crowded room. There was barely enough room to squeeze past the craft tables full of residents and their bingo card collections. He spotted Gus who shouted about how close he was to winning. Herman swallowed hard, knowing good and well he'd not get the man to leave until he did win. Even then, it was iffy. Most gamblers had some luck. Gus didn't, which made him strangely more hopeful than most, insisting the law of averages was on his side.

A well-coiffed head to the left looked familiar. Lola gave him a finger wave. Excellent. Not only was she close to the door, she didn't appear that committed to the game. He hunched his shoulders and bent his knees trying to make himself as small as possible as he weaved through the crowd. In his mind, he imagined he was working his way behind enemy lines, and every glare was a bullet directed his way. It was about as close to actual warfare as his posting in Panama and a lot like this with people sitting around playing games and waiting. Of course, they'd played poker and drank something a little stronger than iced tea, while their job was to keep the canal open, at least for the Allied Forces.

When he got to Lola, he whispered into her ear. "Secret meeting at Marcy's room. Go now."

Lola gave him a wink. "Got it. Have you told Jake?"

"Not yet. Is he here?" He kept his voice low as he searched the room full of white and grey heads for Jake's shiny black pate. He used to take offense at young people joking that old people all looked alike. With their heads down, most did.

"No. Didn't come. Had a book he wanted to finish. I can tell him."

"Sounds good." Extracting Gus would take both gumption and trickery. He made sure to whisper directly into her ear, "Remember, one at a time."

How in the world could he get Gus to leave? Out of the three of them, Gus imagined himself a ladies' man. He used flattery the way some of the residents used cologne—heavily. The result often ended up being a few of the women imagined he had an interest in them he didn't. Gus joked that he kept his flirting to the women in E wing since they were too far away to find him. The man probably lied to them, too, saying he was in a different wing than he actually was.

Plan in mind, Herman squeezed between tables and would have sworn someone patted his butt, but that could have been an accident. Finally, he reached Gus, who was rubbing his hands together and giggling. "I can taste that five-pound box of chocolates."

Herman wasn't even sure if Gus liked chocolate, but it would make him popular with the ladies. He offered bonbons to the women as if the king dispensing favors.

Herman tried to put on a worried face by imagining Eunice finding out about the meeting, which made his hands sweat. This must be what they meant by method acting. He leaned close to Gus and whispered. Nothing.

He tapped on Gus's shoulder for his attention. Aware that he wouldn't hear him in the noisy room, he used sign language, of a sort. He held his cupped hands near his chest, then pointed to Gus, who grinned, apparently not getting the gist of the message he was trying to convey. He held out his left hand and motioned, putting a wedding ring on it—then pointed to Gus who emphatically shook his head.

Herman nodded his head, not sure if he was making progress when Gus stood, darted through the tables, and headed for the door. At least the man was out of the room. Being of the larger persuasion, it wasn't as easy for Herman to squeeze through the tables. Some he had to circle around. When he was almost at the door, he intercepted the interested gaze of Eunice. *Drat.* Better not rush out, or she'd follow him. He paused by her chair and made sure to mention the lack of cards.

"No problem." She patted an empty chair beside her. "I have enough cards for both of us."

Chapter Five

HERMAN MOVED AS fast as he could without breaking out into an outright jog with the sensation of eyes burning holes into his back. A quick glance assured him that no one was paying attention. He left Eunice back in the Bingo room after suffering through several calls. Marcy's room was up ahead, and the door was closed. Indecisive, he stood with his hand raised. Had they decided on a secret knock?

Jake swung the door open. "It's about time. We've been waiting forever. Figured Christmas would show up before you did."

"Very funny. You were here, safe and comfortable. I was cornered by Eunice Ledbetter. Count yourself lucky."

Lola shot him a sympathetic look. "What happened?"

"I was trying to get Gus out of the room."

The man in question looked up. "You said something about wanting to marry me. Didn't know you felt that way. Jake found me in the hallway. You don't feel that way, do you?"

He thought *that*! "Of course not. I happen to know all your bad habits. I was trying to think of a way to get you moving."

"It worked!" Gus declared, making the rest of them laugh.

Marcy rolled forward and handed Herman a sheaf of papers. "This is your copy of the notes. Even though this is a cold case, there are still rules about the information being disseminated to the general public. Lance, who handed me the cases, could be in trouble if it got out that the residents of Greener Pastures were viewing the facts. Think of yourselves as specialized consultants. Read over the notes and let me know if anything sticks out to you."

Lola perched her reading glasses on her nose and made a few muttered replies that may have been more to herself than anyone else. Marcy sniffed and peered at the men.

"Forgot my readers," Jake admitted with a sheepish smile.

Knowing that the focus would soon be on him, Herman started scanning the notes, realizing the location and names would mean nothing to him. Still, as part of a team, he had to try. The rattle of paper had him looking up.

Gus brandished his notes. "What's this about reading? I thought I was here to either explode something or find an unexploded mine or something."

No one would tell him that it was better to have him where they could see him as opposed to letting him roam the center, causing who knows what trouble. Marcy managed a bright smile as she explained. "We do need your superior observation skills. They kept you alive in dangerous situations. What did you look for in those times?"

Gus put his fist to his chin. His eyes rolled up as he tried to dial back the years. The four of them waited for Gus to review a mental record only he was privy to. Finally, he dropped his hand and eyes. He inhaled deeply before speaking. "It feels like a hundred years ago. My training wasn't all that much. It boiled down to two things. No, make that three. Look for things out of place. That could be something as simple as a dry tree branch when it just rained. That signaled someone had brought it along to hide something. The second was to trust my gut."

He held up one finger and waited to make sure he had everyone's attention. "Early man survived by heading the other way when something didn't feel right."

It sounded like Gus got a little more training than Herman. Although Herman did remember his gunnery sergeant urging him to go with his gut. "What was the third thing?"

"Expect something bad if there are strangers nearby watching. Figure they may have witnessed the planting of a mine."

"That makes sense," Herman agreed. "How are we going to know if something is out of place in a crime that's happened a couple of decades ago?"

Marcy held up a manila envelope. "We have pictures."

Instead of opening the envelope, she placed it unopened back in her lap. "I want you to read the notes first. Get in the head of the detective before looking at the photos."

"That's what *you* want," Herman suggested, "but won't it make us unduly prejudiced to think the way the detective thought? The fact that the case hasn't been solved proves he didn't gather enough information to make a case. How about we look at the photos, take our own notes, and then review the detective's?"

"I'm not sure." She cut her eyes to Herman, then inhaled deeply. "I didn't want to redo what has already been done. I didn't want to waste time."

Gus cleared his throat. "You do realize two decades have passed. Not sure what the hurry is."

"Yeah. You're right. Before I show you the pictures, let me warn you they're graphic."

Jake and Gus blustered about being in the war and seeing worse. No need for Herman to remind people he served in Panama, and the only shooting that took place was when a local guard shot himself in the foot after a few rum shots too many. While he enjoyed his post in Central America, it didn't strike the same heroic note as being hunkered down in the mud behind enemy lines.

"Ohhh…" Lola stretched out the word but kept her eyes on the photo. "Just as I suspected."

The rest of them turned their combined faces back to the bloody image that only took a second to overwhelm. Had he missed something? It didn't take a deep study to realize the majority of the woman's face was missing. Jake and Gus looked at him as if they knew what caused Lola's reaction. As a seasoned crime solver, he should, but he didn't. His shoulders went up in a shrug. When he came to lives ended before their time, he played a long game, which worked for cold cases. He just needed more time to consider everything.

"What's the *oh* about?" Marcy asked the question the rest of them were afraid would display their ignorance of a crime-solving detail they'd missed.

One of Lola's manicured fingertips tapped the glossy photo. "You mentioned the woman was a popular socialite."

"Yes." Marcy agreed but looked as perplexed as the rest of them.

"You also said her husband was a wealthy businessman."

Marcy settled for nodding.

"Okay, then." She gestured to the photo. "I may not have had the opportunity to be a trophy wife, but a few of my co-workers did snag that option. What I learned from them is when you're in a certain social bracket you never let people forget it."

"So?" Herman knew this was supposed to be making sense at some level, but he wasn't sure if it was his or Lola's memory that was slipping. It could possibly be both.

Lola picked up the photo and waved it, causing the men to take a step back, rather than stare at the graphic imagery again. "Look at it." She pulled a magnifying glass out of her pocket. "Thank goodness I carry this with me. It helps with the crossword puzzles that for some reason contain print in microscopic font."

Using the glass, she bent over the photo. "Yes. That's what I thought I saw. Just wanted to make sure."

"What?" Gus pushed forward to stare at the photo. "She's such a bloody mess. I'm surprised you can notice anything about what she's wearing."

"It's not what she's wearing. It's what she isn't wearing." She directed a pitying glance toward Gus, who shot an aggravated one right back.

The magnifying glass and photo were passed around as each person had a chance for an up-close viewing. In the photo, he recognized the turned legs of a nearby chair as Chippendale, which could be pricey if it were original as opposed to a reproduction. The bloody, ruined oriental carpet appeared expensive, too. A shock of hair that escaped the blood and gore identified the woman as a blonde. It made him wonder if that was how they identified her, or did they go with she was the only person in the house? Maybe they relied on dental records.

Not getting any replies to her provocative statement, Lola illuminated them. "Women of her social set and age wear their jewels like matrimonial medals showing years served. More like years survived when many wealthy men are quick to replace their wives. It's to remind everyone of their status, considering they no longer have the tight bodies that the younger wives flaunt. Some may have had some work done, but it's hard to get everything done, especially at the same time. What I noticed missing was her jewelry. Nothing. Not even a wedding ring."

"Mmm," Marcy murmured as she directed the magnifying glass

over the photo. "You're right. My family wasn't wealthy, but my mother did attend a few fundraisers that Sue Ellen put on. Apparently, she had a good heart and was raising money for the animal shelter. She had an incredible love for dogs."

"Did she have a dog?" Jake asked.

Herman felt the question was apropos to nothing.

"I don't know." Marcy grimaced. "There's much I don't know about this case. I do know she had this huge blue diamond engagement ring. My mom commented on it, saying it was the size of a robin's egg. I know that was an exaggeration, but it had to be worth plenty."

"That's what I mean." Lola clapped her hands together. "Sue Ellen was dressed for the day. She would have had her jewelry on, especially her engagement and wedding rings."

It looked like the pieces were starting to come together. "That means it could have been robbery."

"There's that." Marcy agreed. "If so, why wasn't it reported as such? I'm sure the ring would have been heavily insured. A ring that size would have been noticeable if it showed up on the jewelry black market. I'm not sure if that was ever investigated."

"What about her dog?" Jake queried while Lola pointed to the photo.

"Did you notice her feet? With the magnifying glass, it appeared as if she had some type of hair on her dark socks.

Before Herman could reply with his own astute observation, Eunice opened the door without bothering to knock. "I wondered where everyone went to. I hoped you didn't start the meeting without me."

Jake and Herman turned to face their unexpected guest, allowing Marcy time to collect the photos and hide them. Gus jumped into the pregnant pause.

"We were *not* having a garden club meeting."

A slight lift of her pencil-enhanced eyebrow announced her disbelief. "What were you doing behind a closed door? I heard Jake mention feet."

Most people would not have opened a closed door, but then there was Eunice. When it came to fast thinking, Herman was not king. Maybe Gus would come up with something. Spinning yarns was another specialty of his. The man looked around as if he was afraid someone might overhear him. The only person he needed to worry about stood about a foot from him. With an index finger held to his lips to indicate secrecy, Gus waited for Eunice's nod before starting.

"We were planning a dance club. Something to liven this place up."

"Good going!" Eunice punched Gus's shoulder hard enough to make him wince. "How far have you got?"

Even though no one had truly discussed dancing, there was a flurry of answers.

"Big Band Revival," Herman quipped, rather proud that he could come up with something quickly.

"Square Dance," Marcy volunteered. "You can do it with a wheelchair."

"Dance lessons." Jake joked out. "We need to start with dance lessons."

"How about burlesque?" Lola teased, causing Eunice to push out one bony hip and place her hand on it in a provocative pose.

"That's something I've always wanted to try. I was afraid the director would put the kibosh on that. I'm willing to help. You might not know it, but I was a great dancer when I was younger."

"Swing?" Jake asked, going with the most obvious era.

"Oh, no." She held her hands out from her sides and pointed one toe, then shuffled and sang about the Good Ship Lollipop. She made a wobbly turn and finished with shaking her hands. "Ta-da! If I were born earlier, I would have given Shirley Temple a run for her money."

Lola, who was still seated and missed most of the questionable performance, asked. "You would have done what to Shirley Temple?"

Before Eunice could answer, Gus did.

"She would have tackled that poor girl. The demonstration I just witnessed bore no resemblance to dancing whatsoever."

"You!" Eunice launched herself at Gus, slamming him with her pocketbook.

"Ouch! Ow! What do you have in that?" he asked behind upheld hands as he attempted to defend himself.

The right thing would be to rescue Gus. It would only be a reprieve. The man would open his mouth again and eventually do something that would get him back into trouble. Herman's feet inched toward the door as if they had a mind of their own.

"Stop it!" Marcy's strong command froze even Eunice in her tracks. Noticing she had everyone's attention, she continued using her hands in a shooing motion. "Everyone out. Now!"

Herman was already at the door and was the first to exit and hot-foot it to his room before Eunice could ask his opinion on her dance performance. One of the things he did learn as a kid was leave before you get in trouble. That advice from his grandfather had served him well.

Chapter Six

THE SUPPLY CLOSET at the end of the hall might have been regarded as good sized, but that was probably with only one person using it or at the most, two. Marcy tried to inch back her wheelchair to accommodate Lola and her walker. The move created a cascade of towels that covered her.

"Here, let me help." Herman lifted the towels off her and handed them to Gus who threw them over his shoulder, hitting Jake in the face.

"Hey, watch what you're doing!"

"Hush! The whole reason we're meeting in the closet is to be secret. That Eunice is a regular bloodhound. It won't take much for her to sniff us out."

Wasn't that the truth. Marcy speculated on how tough the woman would have been to snag if she turned to crime as opposed to nosiness. Probably would have given the police a run for their money.

The five of them shuffled in the tight space, trying to establish some personal boundaries when a mop became unmoored and almost hit Lola.

"This is crazy!" Lola gestured to the mop.

Marcy mentally agreed but wasn't up to forming any new committees. She was already on a first name basis with the activity director, whose name was Irene, due to the gardening club. "It is what it is. We needed someplace secret to meet. Someplace Eunice isn't."

Something else bumped on a shelf, and Herman ended up rubbing the back of his head. "This is like trying to stick ten pounds of potatoes into a five-pound bag. We could go somewhere outside the center. I still have my car."

"That's right." Jake rubbed his hands together. "We could actually go get something edible instead of that slop they've been calling food for a change. Wouldn't feed that to my pigs, if I had pigs.

The whisper of paper drew their attention to Gus as he unfolded a piece of paper. He held up a crudely drawn map. "If we're going out, maybe we can take a drive by the victim's house."

An uneasy feeling pulled on the hairs on the back of her neck. Most cops claimed to have a gut feeling when something bad was about to happen, and hers was ringing, as if bringing in the New Year. "I'm not sure if that is such a good idea. I recall not all of you have the same freedom as Herman."

"True." Jake acknowledged. "If we're not gone very long, no one will notice, as long as we're back before dinner."

"That would work."

"Let's do it."

The elderly crime solvers grinned and jostled everyone as they mapped out their adventure. It looked as if she'd lost control. There had to be a way to put on the brakes of what was bound to be a disaster in the making. "We can't go. I'm in a wheelchair."

The group regarded her as if she had just stated she was a duck. Finally, Jake responded. "What does that have to do with anything?"

"It's hard going anywhere with a person in a chair."

Lola patted her walker frame. "It's probably no different than traveling with a walker. You get in the car. Someone folds up the walker, or in your case the chair, and puts it in the trunk."

The former showgirl's practical explanation shot her argument down. She could refuse to go, which might stop the impromptu trip.

Gus wiggled his way into the center of the group waving his map. "We could go knock on the door where Sue Ellen lived and ask to see inside. That happened to me once while sitting down to dinner. The former owner came by and wanted to go through the house for old time's sake."

"You let him in?" Marcy asked.

"It was a *her,* and I did."

Gus's open face made her wonder how the man ever survived the war, being so trusting. His guardian angel had to be overworked. Nowadays, if someone knocked on a private home and asked for a tour of their previous home, a gun in the face would be a more likely response. If she didn't go, Gus would be knocking on various doors and giving out information he shouldn't. It would all find its way back to the commissioner. Not only would she be in trouble, but Lance, the source of these cold cases, would, too.

"Okay, okay. Let's do it. We'll have to be discreet."

Herman held up his hand as if in class and waited for Marcy to nod in his direction.

He dropped his hand and smiled at the group. "I need to go get my keys. Normally, I go run my car for a bit each week. That way carbon doesn't build up in it. Today, I'll tell them I'm going to get some gas."

"Good idea," Lola volunteered and patted his hand.

Jake cleared his throat and rubbed his chin. "You do realize we can't leave the way we did before. They put up a new camera there."

A derisive snort greeted the announcement. Lola pressed her hand against her chest and patted her eyes. "I don't have the reputation you guys have. I'm going outside to get a little sun. I do that on a regular basis. No one will be suspicious. Marcy can go with me. She doesn't have any wild ways to live down, either."

"That just leaves us," Jake said, glancing back at Gus.

"What?"

Jake turned around to fully face his friend. "I said that just leaves us!"

"No, it doesn't." Gus gave an impish smile. "It just leaves you. Once they put up that new camera, the staff members who smoked had to find a new door to duck out to grab a cig. I happen to know what door that is. Do you?"

"No." Jake lifted his brows some. "You're going to tell me, right?"

"Nah, I'll just let you use all those secret skills you're always alluding to."

Voices outside in the hallway sounded like the custodians. "Give me a minute, I need to grab some cleanser for the lobby bathroom sinks."

Their eyes met one another's, certain they'd be caught in the closet. Jake picked up a can of cleanser and handed it to Lola who was closest to the door. The door swung open about six inches and Lola shot her arm out, holding the cleanser.

The custodian took it from Lola's hand and laughed. "Oh my goodness. I'm not even asking."

"Just as well because I'm not telling." Her response caused the custodian to laugh even harder. "Just hope I have as much life in me if I end up here."

Lola pushed the door closed as opposed to answering. Custodial closets would not work as meeting places. They waited in silence until they were sure the amused housekeeper had moved on. First, Lola popped out, then Herman, followed by Gus who had Jake sticking to him because he hadn't figured out what secret exit the smokers utilized.

Marcy rolled her chair out last and headed for the front lobby. She and Lola would be the bold ones. They'd have to make their move when the shift wasn't changing. Too bad she hadn't told everyone to synchronize their watches. If they all had cell phones, they should be all the same time.

Staff members greeted her in the hall. Doing her best to act casual, she returned their greetings and casual inquiries. A gaggle of uniformed staffers ahead meant there was a staff change. This could work to their advantage if they timed it right. Plenty of cars would be leaving the parking lot. One more wouldn't matter much. The exterior doors had a push button opening system that allowed the wheelchair residents relative ease in exiting or entering. That shouldn't be an issue. Things were going better than she expected. No flashing alarms or anxious staff members running in her direction. Maybe it could work.

The mobile residents who had a good sense of what was going on were usually left to entertain themselves. It wouldn't surprise her if there were a few who left for a stroll or something more. Just when she pushed the door button, a voice reached her.

"There she is!"

How did they know what she was up to? Maybe the custodian had been listening at the door and alerted others. Instead of an agitated floor nurse, Eunice pulled a beleaguered looking activity director behind her.

The red-faced woman gave a huff as she reached the wheelchair. The doors slammed shut before Marcy could exit. Eunice smiled, then prodded her. "Tell her about your dance club ideas."

She hated it when perps played the same card with her. Her jaw dropped as she blinked a couple of times. "What dance club?"

Chapter Seven

MARCY AND LOLA hurried down the pathway, trying to make it to Herman's car without attracting too much attention. The folks coming up the walk gave them a smile and a head nod but posed no questions. The bright sunlight made Lola wish she'd thought to grab her sunglasses. No telling where they were. She had little occasion to use them since retiring from sunny Vegas.

The passenger window lowered, and Gus stuck his head out. "Come on, ladies. We don't have all day!"

Someone inside the car grumbled about him being quiet. The trunk popped open the same time Jake exited the car. He opened the rear door with a flourish.

"Allow me." He held out his hand to Lola. She took it and slid across the upholstery to the middle. He folded up the walker and stowed it in the trunk, then turned to Marcy. She waved him off.

"I can do it myself." Marcy rolled closer to the open car door, secured the brake on her chair, and boosted herself into the back seat. "It's not like I can't stand. I just can't do it for long periods of time."

Herman glanced over his shoulder. "All the more reason you should come. You got in the car faster than Gus did."

"Hey!" Gus puffed up like a banty rooster and blustered. "It was those new-fangled car locks. I'm willing to bet you had it locked."

Herman chuckled but didn't answer the accusation. Instead, he addressed Jake who scooted into the back seat and closed the door.

"Everything good?"

"Yes. Let's hit it."

The car jerked into motion, then crept out of the parking lot. Jake slapped the back of the driver's seat. "Get a move on."

Before Herman could respond, Marcy did. "I think he's doing the exact right thing. No one would be speeding around a nursing home parking lot. That type of reckless driving would attract attention and possibly get the police called."

Jake huffed and grumbled to himself before slumping back into the seat. An uncomfortable silence stretched into a few minutes until the sound of a radio disc jockey filled the car. The sound of rap music had Gus grumbling.

"Not that. I know there's a good station. Heard it in my room. It had all the 1940s hits and a few late ones by ol' blue eyes himself." He fiddled with the controls, causing Herman to fuss.

"Will you leave it alone. No one wants to hear that."

"That's why I'm changing the station." He settled on a warm female voice singing about seeing someone soon. "Woo-wee! I found it."

The song grew suddenly louder in the backseat. Marcy did concert security once for the extra money. Instead of love ballads, it was more classic rock and about as close to bursting her eardrums as this music was. "Turn it down!"

The car swerved as Herman yelled. "Let me do it!"

"No. I'm tired of you treating me like a child."

The music actually got painfully louder, then nothing. Even the silence sounded loud due to the cessation of music being abrupt.

"I'll be." The awe in Herman's voice had Jake leaning forward to peer into the front seat.

"What happened? I see Gus is in one piece, which is more than he would be with me."

The car turned out of the parking lot and progressed through a neighborhood, the destination being the county road most drivers didn't use. The speed dropped even more as Herman explained. "I can turn off the radio with the buttons on the steering wheel. Gwen showed me how to do it, but I never even tried until now. Gus was being such a horse's rear end."

The man in question played with the electric window, buzzing it down and up, causing Herman to sigh. "You can't be doing that, especially on the highway."

No response.

Hardly out of the center parking lot and tempers were already flaring. It reminded Marcy of working at the station. Most people who wanted to be peace officers were decent people with good motives, but it didn't mean they necessarily got along. People might think women were fussy or likely to fly off the handle at a wrong remark. Those people never had to work in close quarters with radio car teams. A good partner made your life easier. One you didn't connect with made it miserable.

"I'm sure you heard me."

Nothing again. Not sure how they could solve a crime when a car ride might result in a brush-up before they even hit the county road. She needed to do something fast. Marcy leaned forward enough to tap Gus on the shoulder. The man left off playing with the window long enough to turn and grin at her.

"What can I do for you, pretty lady?"

Her initial impulse to tell him to stop taunting Herman would only cause him to needle the driver even more. It was time to use her much-vaunted psychology that not only helped her solve numerous cases, but also allowed her to defuse two hostage situations. Surely, she could outsmart one obstinate senior citizen. With his eyes on hers, she enunciated slowly, making sure there would be no mistake about her instructions.

"I know both you and Jake are locals. I need you to pay attention to the road signs while remembering the layout of the city and your notes. The husband in the case claimed not to be at home. It would be good to gauge the length of time it took him to arrive once the housekeeper found Sue Ellen."

"Aye, will do, Captain." He gave a brisk salute, turned back to face the front.

At least she put out that fire. A masculine throat clearing had her turning her head in Jake's direction. He coughed, then inclined his head as if she should know what he meant. His eyes cut to the back of Gus's head, then back to hers.

Men. Was there ever a time they weren't competing with each other? When the hospital transferred her to Greener Pastures for her rehab, she'd been in no real condition to comment about much. A tiny part of her gave a relieved sigh, foolishly thinking the retirement center would be all naps and large print books and the daily head-butting between competitive males would be a memory. Obviously, she thought wrong.

"I'll need everyone's help." No reason to have Lola or Herman complaining she hadn't mentioned them.

Jake held two fingers to his temple as if a signal from his military service or even boyhood days. "Got it. How long did it take?"

How long did it take? Did he just say that? Did she not sneak around and copy the file notes compromising case protocol? She blew out an audible breath. "Did any of you read the notes?"

The car fell silent. Lola arched her eyebrows, pursed her car-mine-red lips, then spoke. "Eight minutes. Seems fast to me as if he were waiting for the call. Notes said he was at work."

"Yes, an early start wasn't unusual for a driven businessman and is probably why he was so successful."

The former Vegas showgirl gave a derisive snort, announcing her feelings about the alibi. "I'm more interested in the housekeeper. Did she live there? Did she also cook? Maybe she served Sue Ellen a power breakfast of coffee and an egg white omelet. Been my experience that those with bucks do as little as possible on their own."

A similar thought had crossed Marcy's mind. The socialite had supposedly been alone at the time of her death. It seemed odd to her, her reflections on the matter similar to Lola's, considering how many wealthy people had someone constantly at their elbow to fetch and carry for them.

"There seems to be little said about the housekeeper's place of residence. The notes state she found the body at half-past ten when she entered the house."

Lola placed two fingers to her lips as she thought. "Could be she was grocery shopping or something."

"True." Marcy was willing to accept the possibility. "She could also have driven from her home."

An exasperated sound issued from Lola. "It's hard to say without talking to her."

The car moved slowly through the neighborhood, causing Jake to grumble. "It'll be Christmas before we get anywhere. Where are we going anyhow?"

Before Marcy could answer, Herman did.

"Someplace where it doesn't look like my dinner has been pre-chewed for me. I'm being cautious and not driving like some show-off cowboy I could name. There are children in this neighborhood"

Jake gave a grunt as his initial reply, then added with a pleased look. "They're in school."

"Not all of them. Haven't you heard of homeschooling?"

Speaking of children, she wanted to clap her hands to put a stop to the bickering. Before she could, Lola placed two fingers in her mouth and emitted a piercing whistle. The men stopped in mid-sentence.

"Now that I have your attention," Marcy started, "I need you to put aside your petty disagreements. You have to want to help Sue Ellen more than you want to fight. If it's important for you to be the head rooster, you can stay at the home, play bingo, and pet the poodles in dresses. If you want to help, you need to follow orders."

There were a few shared glances between the four. The threat of kicking them out was a toothless one. She needed their help, especially Herman's, who owned the wheels. Jake and Gus were familiar with the area. Lola was a student of human nature and had already shown the most promise as an investigator.

At least they acted properly chagrined. Gus turned in his seat and gave the three of them a quizzical look. "What's up with the three of you? You're acting like you farted in church and don't want it pinned on you."

So much for making an impression.

Before Marcy could say anything, Lola piped up. "Weren't you listening? Marcy told us if we didn't act right and help out poor Sue Ellen, it would be back to playing bingo and ducking Eunice."

"Not that!" He winced. "What do we have to do to avoid that?"

"Help with the case without fighting with each other."

The man worked his jaw back and forth as if loosening it to say something. It would probably be something about him not starting the fight. Instead of his usual mischievous smirk, Gus looked thoughtful.

"I did read the notes. I'm not a detective, but I have watched a few crime shows. The thing that stuck out most about the case is how little they did. There wasn't even an explanation of why the woman would commit suicide."

"I noticed that, too, especially considering the woman was a busy, important individual. She could have been receiving counseling, but nothing was mentioned. It's peculiar. If she had been seeing a psychiatrist, the husband would have said so. Right now, we need to move on to where to eat."

"Madeline's!" Jake interjected. "It's a great little café."

Gus shook his head slowly. "They tore that down years ago. There's a balloon shop there now."

The disappointment of her seatmates radiated through the vehicle. It made Marcy a little sad, wondering how far away she was from her favorite places becoming something else. "I thought we could just get sandwiches and go to a park to eat."

There was a general murmur of agreement, which meant they were on the same page—at least for a few seconds.

Chapter Eight

J AKE'S UNHELPFUL ADVICE suddenly stilled as Herman pulled onto the county road. The rearview mirror showed his buddy hadn't fallen out of the car or was asleep as his silence might have suggested. Instead, he peered out the window at the passing scenery as if memorizing it. Come to think of it, Jake had shown quite an interest in the various homes, farms, and railroad tracks as they'd made their way to North Carolina.

A blur of color and a spritely *beep* startled Herman causing him to slow down as a scooter whipped around him.

Gus shook his fist at the back of the helmeted rider. "Those things shouldn't even be on the road."

Herman seconded the sentiment and took a deep breath, glad that a careless swerve hadn't been his reaction to the beep. Back in Legacy, he drove maybe once a week. That was different. He knew the streets there. By going anywhere between eleven and two, he avoided the school buses and rush hour. Unwilling to admit his unease, he chose to tease Jake. "You act like you never get out of the home."

The man grunted, not willing to discuss the subject. Lola wasn't as reticent. "Where would we go? The activities director doesn't arrange trips anymore. I heard her say it was more trouble than buckling toddlers into car seats."

"That's a little harsh." Marcy commented. "The wheelchairs and walkers might be a bit of trouble, but we pay good money to stay here. It wouldn't hurt for us to have a weekly outing."

How long had he been here? Two-three months, maybe more—he wasn't sure. He had taken the unauthorized road trip a few weeks after he arrived. A month or so ago, he went to a family reunion that resulted in another visit to Legacy to check out a skeleton that could have been the basis of his favorite local legend. Here, he came out on a weekly basis to start his car and an employee rode with him to help him locate a gas station. On the way, they stopped for pizza and Herman paid. The employee claimed to have forgotten his wallet. Sounded suspicious to Herman, but he'd pay to get something a little tastier than mystery meat. It never occurred to him that no one else ever left the center. "No one goes anywhere?"

"Seriously?" Jake issued a derisive snort, signaling his thoughts on the matter.

"Look at that!" Gus shouted, causing heads to turn in various directions.

Worried another scooter was about to pass him, Herman inquired with concern, "What is it?"

"A 57 Chevy. It was underneath us on the highway." Gus pointed with his right hand in the direction the car had been. "Cherry condition."

Herman was thankful they weren't sharing the same road. The only person in the car who had current knowledge about the streets would be the youngest. "Marcy, am I going the right way?"

Before she could answer, Jake butted in. "There's no way you could tell the year of the car from this distance."

For a man who missed most remarks, Gus responded to one that attacked one of his remaining senses. "I know what I saw. You're just sorry your weak eyes didn't see it."

"My eyes aren't weak."

"Kept you from being a flyboy."

"Not true."

Herman, never having children, had no opportunity to experience family road trips, but he imagined they sounded a lot like this. "Don't make me turn this car around." He couldn't help chuckling at the sudden cessation of bickering. "You do realize we'll miss out on eating something recognizable and won't get to help on the case. We'll end up being useless senior citizens that are apparently more trouble than toddlers to take anywhere."

"Knock it off guys." Lola added. "I didn't leave Vegas to be warehoused in some home."

A speed sign on the right reminded him the speed limit was forty-five, which caused him to glance at the speedometer. *Thirty.* No reason to speed up, considering he didn't know where he was going, and there was no one behind him. He had moved to the center for companionship, but he'd been second-guessing the decision ever since. If he hadn't sold his house for a nice bit of change, he'd have hightailed it back to Legacy and all that was familiar. "Why'd you leave Vegas?"

"It's a young person's town. For a while, I worked as an office manager at an insurance company once I hung up my feathers. Did it longer than my showgirl job. I used to love to go down to the strip and watch the shows. They've changed over the years. Not as much elegance as there used to be. I felt like that old Gloria Swanson movie where the silent movie star lived in the past. A co-worker was planning on retiring back in Indiana, and she was tired of the desert. I never even visited the state, but she made it sound peaceful and green. My decision to accompany my friend was impulsive, but it had to be better than visiting the strip and telling all the tourists I used to be a backup dancer at the Flamingo. Most whispered I was a crazy old coot. Some said it to my face. I figured it was time to go."

The five of them were quiet, possibly mourning the lives they'd left behind. Marcy spoke first. "Turn right at the stop sign. It will take us up to an area with a lot of fast food places. We can grab something from the drive-thru, then hit the park."

Herman clicked on his right turn signal about an eighth of a mile from the stop sign. It was better to be prepared, instead of wildly veering right. Lola's story stayed with him, making him wonder if he had been a bit like that. Had he always been talking about the past to anyone who would listen? "What happened to Irene?"

No reply, which made him wonder if she even heard him. A peek in the mirror revealed a knitted brow, then she answered. "She died."

"I'm sorry."

The normally bubbly woman gave a heavy sigh. "We all die sometime. None of us are immortal. I guess I would have expected her to live a little longer. That's all. She died six months after we moved here. By that time, I'd cut all my ties to Vegas. No real family to speak of, so I stayed. That's been—let me see—six years ago. Six long years. I need something to keep my mind functioning, or I will be the dotty old female the tourists thought I was."

"Understand." Herman acknowledged as he slowed for a railroad track and crept over it. No need to ruin his suspension system. Had he made people doubt his sanity when he went on and on about the missing jewels story? If so, no one told him.

He had to press the pedal down to get the car to climb the hill without slowing too much. The farm fields, a dance studio, and a greenhouse gave way to a forest of store signs advertising everything from gasoline to Chinese food.

"Take a gander, crew." Marcy announced. "Lunch is out there somewhere. I'm picking up the tab. Nothing too pricey and we have to be able to get it from the drive-thru window. It's not worth wrestling my wheelchair out of the trunk to go in. Besides, we need to be somewhere we can be discreet."

Jake nodded. "Covert reconnaissance mission."

"Not quite, but there's no reason for people to know our business. We can head out to the park and maybe eat at one of the picnic tables."

"I'm not sure if Crackers has a drive-thru. I guess they might."

Not that again. Jake could remember things that happened years ago in perfect detail, much better than Herman. Unfortunately, his memory sometimes failed to update to the current day.

Marcy met his eyes in the rearview mirror and gave a slight nod. "Jake, Crackers sounds like a wonderful place, but it isn't on this street. We have burgers, fish, and tacos to pick from."

After some spirited discussion, they decided on a burger joint that also served burritos and fish sandwiches.

Marcy directed him from the back seat. "Turn here."

"Here where?" There was a half-dozen entrances to his right.

"Home Boy, red and yellow sign with the goofy guy on it."

He turned on his signal and made a mental apology to the car behind him for making such a sudden turn as he moved into the entrance. *Okay, he was here.* "What now?"

"Get in line for the drive-thru."

The woman said it as if he knew what she meant. He understood the concept of the drive-thru. Gwen, his great-niece, had even driven him through a few on their latest trip together. His experience was they seldom got the order right. He never actually drove through one by himself. Arrows painted on the pavement along with the words DRIVE THRU helped him find his way. He flicked on his turn signal just to warn anyone behind him where he was heading.

A car idled in front of a colorful lighted sign that sprouted out of a raised concrete strip. The motorist yelled at the sign about a *Home Boy Special* with a *Your Momma* shake. Herman knew what to do. All he had to do was drive up there and yell out some food selections. Easy-peasy. A left-handed pull on the wheel put him somewhat closer to the sign.

Jake grumbled. "I can't see what they have."

"You can't see period," Gus tacked on, showing he truly had selective hearing.

"Herman…" Marcy began in a soothing tone she probably used when talking to thugs who had a weapon on her, "You're going to have to move closer for the people to see."

Great. That meant he'd have to back up and start again. No one behind him, which meant he had no real excuse. "Couldn't I just get out and yell into the speaker?"

A backward glance revealed Marcy sucking her lips in. That must be a *no.* He backed up, then put the car into drive, only to find he had three backseat drivers and one passenger driver.

"No! Closer."

"Cut it to the right."

"No, the left."

The driver's side front tire climbed the concrete strip only to have Gus announce, "Too close."

"I noticed." Herman steered the car on the concrete without touching the sign everyone wanted him to be close to. Did anyone notice that major driving skill? Nope. They were all too involved in staring at the menu.

"Where's the frog sticks?" Jake questioned. "Can't have a burger without my frog sticks."

"What?" Lola and Marcy asked in unison.

Herman felt the need to explain and help out his buddy. "Jake, they're called French fries here. Frog sticks were slang for the term *frog* referring to the French, although I have it on good authority fries were actually invented in Belgium."

It took a little more quibbling before they placed their order. Lola asked for extra sauce, while Gus insisted on knowing why they didn't have shamrock milkshakes even if it wasn't St. Patrick's Day. It was hard telling if Gus was serious or just having fun at the fast food worker's expense.

Lunch in hand, they headed off for the park, which was close by. It took less than ten minutes to arrange themselves around a picnic table in a shelter house that had a pothole riddled path.

The tempting smells had them all unwrapping their sandwiches. It looked good to him and tasted even better. It was hard to believe he used to dine regularly at The Painted Lady Inn on gourmet treats. Now, he was chowing down on fast food and counting himself lucky.

Marcy pushed her half-eaten sandwich aside, pulled a writing tablet out of her bag, and clicked a pen. "All right, team, what have we got on this case, so far?"

Lola waved her burrito. "No motivation for suicide. No friends came forward to mention her being depressed. Nothing about her getting therapy. Was there even a note?"

"There was mention of one, but there is no transcript or even a photo of the note. All we have is someone said there was a note. Who was that somebody?"

"My money is on the husband." Jake spoke around a French fry half inserted into his mouth. "It's almost always the spouse. Did he benefit from her death?"

"Not as much as most people might think." Marcy scratched a few words on the tablet. "They had separate wills. Most people make theirs together. One of those things where one person gives the remaining spouse everything and vice versa."

Gus chewed vigorously while watching the interplay. He swallowed, freeing himself to join the discussion. "Did the dame have any money? If so, who got it?"

Using her pen as a conductor's baton, Marcy held it up, engaging their attention. "Sue Ellen did come from an affluent family. After her parents and brother died in a plane crash on their way to their vacation home, she inherited everything. I heard she had a mind for money. Even though she headed up all the animal rescue fund drives, she contributed heavily to them, too. The big winners would have been the Animal Rescue League. Rumor is they got two million dollars."

Gus whistled.

Normally that should cut the husband out as a possible killer. Money was the usual motivator. As the somewhat veteran crime solver, Herman knew Marcy expected him to come up with some good deductive reasoning. "What if the husband didn't know he wasn't the beneficiary?"

"That's good. We'd have to get a copy of the will. Not sure I can do that. Got anything else?"

Lola shook her head. "I keep coming back to the missing jewels. Was an insurance claim filed?"

"There was no robbery reported. You need a police report to file a claim. Otherwise, the insurance company is justifiably suspicious. Everyone would be declaring their valuable gems had been stolen.

Plenty of people do that already, and they have the brass to call the police to make their report look genuine."

Jewels. This was Herman's area. "Could be no paperwork was filed because the husband knows exactly where the jewelry is, especially that fancy engagement ring you mentioned. Find the ring and you'll probably uncover the motive."

Boy, that sounded good! Smiles and head bobs greeted his statement. Marcy wrote a few lines in her indecipherable script. People thought men had bad handwriting.

"Great call. Excellent work all of you. If this ever went to court, it would have been thrown out for lack of evidence. It would be good to know if the husband knew about his exclusion from the will. Better yet, what happened to the jewelry, especially the showy blue diamond. The problem is finding out."

Lola bounced on the hard picnic table bench and waved her left hand. "I know who would know."

Fiddlesticks. That woman thought of everything. She may not have crime-solving experience like him, but she was a primo people watcher. "Who?"

If she said the husband that would be close to useless. If the man was guilty, he wouldn't talk. If he wasn't guilty, no reason to torture an innocent man by mentioning his wife's gruesome demise.

Lola gave him a knowing look as if she knew what he was thinking, then she winked.

"The housekeeper. It's likely the wife would interact with the housekeeper more than the husband. Even when people don't mention personal information to the staff, they know. Servants always know."

"Brilliant!" Marcy clapped her hands together. "I know the woman is still alive. All we have to do is find out where she lives. I might be able to look her up with my phone. See if she is home and make an impromptu visit."

Knowing that people didn't appreciate unexpected guests, Herman had his doubts about the plan. "Shouldn't we make an appointment?"

"Absolutely not. If we call ahead, she could make an excuse not to see us. It also gives her time to contact the husband if she wants to make sure they're on the same page. I'm not saying they're compatriots. Calling your former employer whose wife died might feel like the right thing to do to her. It's best to surprise people into telling the truth."

Marcy dropped her head as she picked out information on her tiny keyboard. "Woo hoo! I found her. Better yet, she lives in a nearby town about thirty minutes from here."

Chapter Nine

THE SLANTING SUNLIGHT picked out the dust motes hovering in the air. It was probably already four. Marcy peeked at her watch. It *was* four. The quick jaunt into the other town took longer than she expected. Herman got lost twice. To be fair to the man, having three people shouting directions at him probably wasn't helpful. Then Gus needed to go to the bathroom.

Here they sat in a gas station parking lot. Truthfully, she could go, but the idea of a nasty public restroom convinced her she could wait. Besides, if they ever made it to Mabel Elliot's house, she could ask to go then. Could she turn down a woman in a wheelchair?

Gus jogged back and climbed into the front seat. "Let's go! There was a line that was out to kingdom come."

"Did you go?" Herman asked the obvious question. Why else would they be baking in a hot car?

"What?"

Instead of repeating the inquiry, he started the car and maneuvered slowly through the busy parking lot. Nearly every pump was occupied, while a few cars waited their turn. A scooter and its driver utilized the air pump while two employees stood nearby chatting with the driver. Teenagers left the minimart, clutching oversized drinks and chips.

Lola swiveled her head and counted the people as the car exited. "I counted twenty-two people. Wouldn't be a big deal in Vegas.

Makes me wonder if this is the only gas station in town."

She addressed the question to Marcy. It would be up to her to answer. It wasn't like she knew the details of every small town in the area, but she did grow up in one nearby—Georgetown. The Hoosier State was dotted with them. Most had a school, a couple of churches, at least one gas station, and an ice cream shop that was open about eight months out of the year. "Could be. It also might be the only activity the residents have."

"You're pulling my leg." Lola wrinkled her nose as if uncertain of Marcy's intentions. "What do people do in small towns?"

"You just saw it. There's the 4-H fair in the summer. Maybe a parade on the Fourth of July. If they're lucky, there'll be a drive-in movie theatre."

"Reminds me of when I was a boy," Jake grinned as if remembering a younger, untroubled time. "I think they tore down the drive-in to put in a strip mall or something. Everywhere you go there are more stores, restaurants, even med checks. I don't think there are enough people in New Albany to make all these places profitable."

Marcy recognized a rant when she heard one, but there wasn't time to listen to how things used to be. "All right, team, we're almost there. Let me do the talking since investigating crimes is what I do for a living. You guys just sit there and look pretty."

It sounded a bit patronizing when she thought about it. Jake pointed to his eyes. "I'll give the place a good look over to see if anything is out of place."

"Um, Jake, you can't stroll about the house as if you're the pet cat. It will take work to get into the house. What we need to know is locked up in Mabel Elliot's brain—not her house."

"Got it." He turned to stare out the car window, making Marcy think he did *not* have it. As far as her crew members went, she'd label Jake the most headstrong. Gus, the most mischievous. Herman, the most willing to please. Lola was her ace in the hole. The woman had the makings of a profiler.

"What if..." Her would be profiler wiggled her ring-laden fingers. "...Mabel stole the ring?"

"It's possible. How would she get rid of it? I doubt she knows any high-end jewelry fences. Even if she did, why would the husband go along with the suicide theory?"

"Makes you wonder." Lola retrieved a compact from her bag and opened it to check her makeup. Satisfied, she stowed it.

The car slowed as it turned onto Water Street. *Almost there.* They crept down the right side of the road, reading house numbers on the tidy homes. At the end of the street was a modest home with a white picket fence around it. "This is it," she instructed Herman, "but don't park here. She could see us coming and lock the door."

He made a loud sigh and made an awkward turn since it was a dead end. The front tire went up on the curb and came down with a bounce. Gus grunted. "Learn to drive."

"Remember, I'm the one with a car, not you." Herman steered the large sedan in front of a house that featured possibly every type of garden gnome known to man. He stopped the car and parked. "We're here. What's the plan?"

Marcy nudged Jake with her elbow. "I'll need you to get my chair. Let's hope there are no stairs or very few."

"Don't worry about it, sweetie." Lola patted her hand and managed a sympathetic look. "If we're visiting a retired woman, I doubt she'd have any steps at all. A woman has to consider her future ability to move around the house. Those chair elevators for two story houses don't work worth crap. I had one. It figured into me making the choice to come to the home. It made me feel older having to strap myself into my easy glide chair. I even worried what I would do if it ran down while I was in the middle of the stairs. Anyone with any sense would live in a ranch house with as few steps as possible."

It took a few minutes for everyone to get out of the car. Marcy had already made it clear with determination to be first at the door. A subtle clicking sound of the wheelchair wheels was the only sound as they made the slow way to Mabel's cottage. The fence gate swung open under Jake's hand, and Marcy maneuvered her chair through it and down the narrow sidewalk. Lola managed to be second in line, next was Gus, then Jake, with Herman serving as the caboose.

A shallow stoop stopped Marcy's progress, causing a domino effect through the whole group. No doubt Jake would run up and be the gentleman. Not this time. Herman jogged around the group and made it to the door before anyone else and knocked.

Nothing. They waited. Maybe he should knock again. His hand was raised to do so when a voice called out from inside. "Hold your horses! I'm on my way."

The door swung open. A robust woman attired in a plaid shirt and Mom jeans gave the group a curious look. She shook her head, and her chin-length bob moved with the motion. "Are you all lost?" Before anyone could answer, she held up her hand as if stopping their progress. "No need for you to go witnessing to me. I have my own church. Sorry for you to go to all the trouble of working your way up my walk. Did they run out of young people to carry the message?"

"No, ma'am..." Marcy started but was interrupted by the chatty woman who used her upheld hand to gesture to the right.

"Jamison down the block could use some help. Three houses

down. His is the yard with nothing in it, rather like the man himself."

"We're here about the Sue Ellen Makowski case."

Mabel's hand dropped, and her eyes narrowed. "What about Sue Ellen? The poor woman has been dead and buried several years now."

"I know. I'm Detective Marcella Collins. I'm on a cold case investigating Sue Ellen's death."

The sound of a door slamming caught their attention. Everyone turned to see a blue-haired lady exiting the house next door with a small yappy dog on the end of a leash.

Mabel snorted. "Oh, for Pete's sake. Come in."

It took them a while to get the entire group into the small living room. Mabel left the room and returned with a straight back chair. "I had to get you in here before that gossip caught wind of your talk. I'm tired of bad talk about Sue Ellen. She deserved much better."

"We agree she deserved better. That's why we're here."

Gus held up his hand and did an awkward dance. "I need to use the facilities."

They had earlier discussed getting into the bathroom to snoop a little bit. He ignored Marcy's head shake and continued to fidget. "I really have to go. The line at the gas station was too long, remember?"

Mabel cut her chin to the left. "John's down the hall." She turned to face the rest of the group. "Explain to me why you're here again? The way I understand it, once a death is confirmed a suicide, it's done."

"True, but there's some suspicion that maybe it wasn't a suicide. That's why the case reopened."

Instead of an immediate response, Mabel paced the center of the living room in the tiny three by five on a floral design carpet. She mumbled to herself. "I knew good and well my Sue Ellen wouldn't commit suicide. It wasn't how she was. I told the police as much, not that it did any good. If they're investigating it, why didn't they send out a regular detective?" She cleared her throat. "No offense."

The words more than ruffled Herman's feathers. Momentarily forgetting his intentions to let Marcy do the talking, he interrupted. "Don't let the hair fool you." He placed both hands on his hips. "I consulted on several murder investigations with success."

"Oh, you're all retired police?" She indicated the rest of the group.

Eyes met, but Jake piped up before anyone else could. "Something like that."

Marcy's head pivoted so hard in Jake's direction it was surprising it didn't fly off. "Ah...that's what we came to talk about. If you could remember anything unusual about the day before Sue Ellen died."

The woman heaved a sigh, then walked over to a chair and collapsed into it. Her shoulders slumped as she settled into her seat. "Didn't seem right, Sue Ellen killing herself, especially when she worked non-stop for the no-kill animal shelters. Why would a woman who couldn't stand to see an unwanted pet killed, kill herself?"

"Makes no sense." Marcy agreed and pulled a small tape recorder out of the messenger bag slung across her body. "Mind if I record?"

"Go ahead." Her face dissolved into morose lines, pulling it downward and aging Mabel another ten years. "I had opinions. Plenty of them, but sometime after I called the police and Mr. Makowski, her husband, no one had much use for what I had to say."

"That's why we're here." Marcy gave her an encouraging nod. "It's time for you to have your say. What did you want to tell the police?"

Her hands covered her face, but she gradually withdrew them revealing a dry, emotion-less face, surprising Herman. The woman was no gentle flower.

"I saw Sue Ellen before her…" her hands went up to make air quotes, "…suicide." She closed the quotes and continued. "She was dressed and was excited, talking about the upcoming conference. It was something about having a marathon sit-in at the shelter. People would pledge money for Sue Ellen and other volunteers for the hours they stayed. She was excited about this. No signs of depression at all."

"Wait. You're saying the police totally ignored you?"

"Not at first, but Mr. Makowski comes wading in with all this talk about depression and her being bi-polar. Even said she was off her meds. One detective kinda listened to me. Later on, I heard it declared a suicide. I'm not even sure if they did an autopsy. Mr. Makowski told me Sue Ellen wasn't right, which caused her to take her own life, when he retired me with a generous severance pay. It allowed me to semi-retire and pursue my dream of writing romance novels."

Her? Writing romance novels? The possibility of this no-nonsense woman writing something all hearts and flowers made Herman chuckle, drawing everyone's attention. "Pardon me." He flushed a little. "I just remembered the punch line to a joke I heard a while back." His cheeks grew even redder, well aware he didn't sound that believable. "It was about a horse that walked into a bar…"

Marcy shook her head, stopping him from elaborating on his lame excuse and redirected the conversation.

"Did you know anything about Sue Ellen being bi-polar?"

"Absolutely not." She shook her head vigorously. "I worked for Sue Ellen for years. I not only kept house, but I kept track of her events. Not on a computer or anything, but there was a big block calendar in the kitchen. Often, I reminded her what was on her plate that day, although she was fairly organized and knew herself. I just liked telling her. I guess it made me feel important." She managed a sad smile.

The plastic covering Lola's chair squeaked as she wiggled on it, barely containing her impatience. Her eyes flashed a warning she'd held her peace about as long as she could. "Ask her about the ring."

Mabel obviously didn't need any prompting. "It wasn't on her hand. I noticed. I should have said something at the time, but I was suspicious. I thought her husband might have killed her. The ring, in my opinion, was the piece of evidence that ties everything together. I waited for a while to see if it turned up, maybe at a pawn shop or something. Didn't really have the resources. I showed up at the pawn shops in town asking about big blue diamonds and got shown a bunch of cubic zirconium crap. I imagine a resourceful person would have headed to a different town, but I'm one woman and can only do so much."

"You suspected the husband?"

"I did. He had an alibi. An eyewitness reported he was at work."

Marcy nodded. "That's what the notes said. Any other reasons you'd suspect him?"

Her shoulders went up in a shrug. "It's a fact that widowers marry sooner than widows. Still, I thought Mr. Makowski moved on very fast."

"He remarried?"

"After one year."

"Good to know."

The group exchanged knowing glances. Herman thought the man sounded guilty, which was usually the plot of most crime shows. Never mind how loving the husband seemed, he was usually guilty. Gus entered the room, talking a little too loudly.

"You'll be relieved to know everything came out okay."

Good grief. Herman closed his eyes, feeling humiliated at his friend's behavior. When he opened them again, Gus was grinning as if he was pleased about something.

Jake held up his arm displaying his watch and pointed at it. What time was it, anyhow? Normally, Herman wore a watch, but he forgot it today. He reached into his pocket and retrieved his cell phone. The cool, slender rectangle that was supposed to be a source of communication consistently baffled him. Something about swiping to the right, which he did. The glowing numbers read 4:45. In no way could they get back to the center on time. He and Marcy shouldn't get much grief since they could come and go as they please—at most, a stern talking to about how they needed to log their visits outside the center and get the proper clearance for it. Jake and Gus were an entirely different matter.

"Guys?" He coughed to get their attention. "It's getting late."

Marcy looked up. "We should get going." She pivoted her chair to face Mabel as opposed to simply turning her head. "I appreciate your help. Could we return to follow up on this conversation? We have another appointment, unfortunately."

"Yes. I'd like to see justice for poor Sue Ellen. I'm glad someone still remembers her. Thank you for looking into the matter."

The crew paraded out with each other thanking Mabel for her

hospitality. Jake made sure to take her hand and look into her eyes. Did the man think he was a vampire and could hypnotize the woman? That's what he'd have to do. The good looks he'd depended on had faded, if not deserted him. Someone should tell the man, but it wouldn't be her. Sometimes, memories were all you have.

The nosy neighbor and her yappy dog stood outside on the sidewalk, unabashedly watching them as they left Mabel's yard.

"You Mabel's relatives?"

Marcy gave the woman a smile. "No, we're friends."

"Interesting. Never saw anyone come around here ever since she moved here. The one exception was her former boss who came by."

The information waved a red flag for sure. Would friends be curious, or would they already know? "Yeah, he's considerate like that. Did he come by recently?"

"No." The woman pursed her lips. "It's been years, I think. Time plays tricks on you sometimes."

It would have been much more helpful if the woman could pin-point a time. A *year* or *years* was a world of difference than *last week*. If the no longer grieving husband was trying to stay on the good side of Mabel Elliot, she could have told him it wasn't working.

They parted from the woman with waves and muttered excuses about needing to hurry. It took less time to enter the car, which worked to their advantage. They needed to get going.

Before Herman could start the car, Gus announced, "Checked out the bathroom. Not much to report, except Mabel has blood pressure medicine and a bottle of antacid. Nothing fancy in the bathroom. None of that expensive salon shampoo. The towel hanging from the shower rod was ragged. No luxuries there. Did she get anything in the will?"

"Good question. We need to investigate this. I can ask Lance about it. There has to be a copy somewhere. It might be enough to request it."

"Sounds like a plan," Jake concurred.

Herman grimaced. He silently mouthed the words, while sneering slightly as he moved into traffic. A yellow school bus pulled out in front of him. *Great.* He'd be forced to putter along the road, making their route back even slower. What else could happen? The bus put out its flashing stop signal sign, forcing Herman to stop and silently fume as kids leisurely exited the bus. By the time the third munchkin with a superhero backpack got off, he had to suck in his lips to keep from shouting, "Hurry up."

A red-faced woman popped out of a nearby house and boarded the bus, delaying the process even more. Finally, the woman reappeared with a triumphant smile as she strolled back to her house. Thank goodness they were able to move again, all five hundred yards to the next stop.

The drive back took all of his concentration. Everyone had instructions on how he should drive, which was usually *faster*. Even if he drove in the Indianapolis 500, he wouldn't be able to make it back to the center in time for dinner. It was the time they counted everyone, since each resident was served a dinner tray either in the dining hall or in their room. An aide would take a covered plastic tray to his room and remove the name card as they served it. No way they would not notice the absence of five residents.

Chapter Ten

LOLA LET OUT a long, relieved breath as Herman pulled into the center parking lot. A beautiful sunset with vivid red and purples colored the sky. Shadows were just starting to form at the edges of the building wings and under the mature oak and maple trees. Fairly soon, the shadows would spread until they united together and created a blanket of darkness.

She turned away from the gorgeous scenery and scanned the long rows of windows. It would be no easy trick getting inside unnoticed. Plenty of residents spent time staring out their windows. A few hoped by doing so they'd get a jump on unexpected visitors with enough lead time to put on some lipstick or run a comb through their hair. The others constantly monitored the comings and goings of the staff members, thoroughly convinced they might pick out a wanted fugitive from the reality crime shows they consistently watched.

If that wasn't bad enough, she knew all the doors were alarmed. A buzz and a light would sound at the nurse's station. She'd seen it happen more than once. If someone was on duty, they usually shouted down the corridor as opposed to sprinting down it. No wonder because it was usually staff leaving to get something out of their cars or sneaking out for a cigarette. The newer staff might check it out though.

"Maybe we should go in separate doors?" Lola floated the idea—

mainly for Marcy. Gus knew his way around the cameras but couldn't hear her sitting in the front seat.

"I agree. Before we go in…" Marcy raised her voice to get everyone's attention, "…have your story ready. Obviously, we won't have the same story. Keep it simple and believable. Many a criminal was tripped up by his convoluted story. Not only are they hard to remember, they just reek of fiction."

There was some general discussion of workable excuses when Herman slammed on the brakes and shouted, "Good heavens!"

Fortunately, their driver couldn't have been going over ten miles per hour. Slamming wasn't too bad, and they all had on seatbelts. The space between Gus and Herman revealed the headlights shining on a woman waving her arms wildly. What in the world?

"Eunice Ledbetter…should have known, or at least expected it. That woman must have radar or something." Herman grumbled. "I could go around her."

"You could," Jake concurred. "It won't stop her from following us. It probably won't stop her from flapping her lips, either. Best to see what she wants. If nothing else, the woman is an opportunist."

The hum of the window going down meant Herman had taken Jake's advice without bothering to run it past the rest of them. Just like a man—at least the ones she knew—always assuming the women didn't have anything significant to add to the discussion. Not entirely true. They were yielding to Eunice. Jake and Herman had had more encounters with the wily individual than she had. It meant they knew when to hold their cards and when to fold while dealing with this particular female.

Eunice stuck her head into the window, causing Herman to lean toward Gus, as if he didn't want to be accused of being indecently close. The open air brought with it a scent of burning leaves and the sound of someone playing a radio way too loud in the nearby neighborhood. If people needed to play music that loud, why not something good like Frank Sinatra or that delicious new guy, Steve Terrell?

"Glad I caught you." Eunice's voice sounded overloud in the car. "Otherwise all the excuses I made up for all of you would be wasted."

"What excuses?" Gus asked, proving that either Eunice was loud enough or that she was close enough to read her lips—or possibly the third option that he could hear just fine and only pretended to be half deaf.

"They're all good and appropriate for your situations. Herman was the easiest. He has a car and the right to drive it wherever he pleases. I mentioned to the dietary aide that you were working on your car. Might even take it out for a spin, too."

"Believable." Herman nodded in her direction.

Jake waved his hand, "How about me?"

"Ah, yes, that was a good one." She chuckled. "A lie needs a grain of truth. Since you usually come to the dining room for dinner, to explain why you didn't, I told the attendant you were sulking because the ladies you were romancing found out about each other and kicked you to the curb."

"What! You didn't."

"I did." Eunice's glasses bounced on her nose as she attempted to wiggle her eyebrows. "Go on and slip into D Wing. The west door is propped open right now to air out the place. Someone burned popcorn in the staff lounge again."

Jake opened his door, making sure to give Eunice a look before exiting and moving to the trunk. Even though she couldn't see Jake's entire face, Lola saw enough to know the man was far from pleased. Herman popped the trunk allowing Jake to do the gentlemanly thing and retrieve the wheelchair and walker. He set both up beside the car before heading in the direction of D wing. Lola knew whatever Eunice had to say she wouldn't like, but she was also curious about Gus and Marcy's excuses.

"As for Marcy..." Their questionable savior cocked her head toward the back seat. "It would be good for you to come in the front. May have let it slip you were outside waiting for a former boyfriend to show up. He didn't, and you didn't want anyone to see you crying."

The woman stiffened beside Lola. "I don't cry. No one will believe that."

"You can get by with more than most since no one expects you to stay all that long. Most of the staff feels sorry for you, anyhow."

"No one needs to feel sorry for me. I'm more capable than most." She swung the car door open, gingerly exited, managed a few swaying steps to her wheelchair, and rolled away.

A surprised silence settled over the remaining three. It felt like they were on some awkward reality show where people got voted off.

Gus broke the silence. "Go ahead and tell me what you've done to me."

"Nothing bad—not really. I told them you were constipated again, and you were in the bathroom."

"Good lord, woman! Can't you leave me some dignity?" He slammed the door as he left.

"Hey!" Herman exclaimed and tried to push Eunice out of the window. "You've made everyone mad, and they're taking it out on my car."

Overall, Lola thought they had reason to be perturbed. The stories were probable even if they tended to be a little dramatic when it came to Jake and Marcy. "Go ahead tell me."

"Everyone knows you love to look your best!"

Yes, she did. Lola held her head up with pride, not sure why everyone was against Eunice. The woman just told things as she saw them.

"Anyhow…" Eunice continued. "I told them you had an emergency beauty shop appointment."

It made her sound petty and superficial, but sadly it was believable. "Any door I should go in?"

"Use the front. It's not alarmed and closest to the beauty shop."

"Thanks. I appreciate your effort." She slid across the seat, released the door, and walked the few steps to her walker. Technically, she could probably have managed it without her walker, but her doctor didn't want her to take any chances. Old bones tended to be brittle. She shuffled the dozen steps to the front entrance wondering when she got to be such an old woman.

Back in Vegas, she fought the good fight, trying to stay reasonably young looking, from going to the gym to having an assortment of Botox and fillers put in her face to make it look like forty wasn't a dim memory. Even though she'd heard some professional football team took on a fifty-year-old cheerleader, it didn't make her think for a second that she'd be back on stage again. No, she didn't want to admit she was getting older and accept all the accompanying baggage that came with it.

The most frustrating part was older people were sometimes invisible. There was a book or a movie out several years ago where some young female journalist dressed up as an old lady for a story. When she was an impoverished old lady, people made a point of avoiding her. When she was a middle-class matron, folks used selective hearing and sight to not interact. Only when she was a wealthy, old broad did people give her the time of day, which was usually only to get a tip or to con her. Since she was far from wealthy that put her in the middle.

The image she had of old people was they watched a lot of television and griped about how good things used to be. Even the television survey companies weren't interested in the fifty and over due to them being too set in their ways. No matter how entertaining a commercial was, it wouldn't make a senior change brands.

Back when she was tapping her high heels and fluffing out her feathers waiting to go on stage, it never occurred to her she'd be here. Some lonely old woman who had as much value as a VCR in a garage sale. Most people would say she brought it on herself due to the fact she never married. She didn't want to marry for the wrong reasons, and most of the offers she got as a showgirl were from married men and not matrimonial ones, either. Later on, there weren't all that many offers and none of them appealed. Sure, she could have had kids. Then they would have put her in the center as opposed to herself. Maybe she was only down on herself. Still, it beat being dead.

Up ahead, she could see the illuminated front porch. The brightness was almost blinding. Did they use searchlight bulbs? Lola squinted to focus as she drew closer to the door. The wheel of a wheelchair caught her eye. Who was sitting out here?

Please, don't let it be one of those confused dears who were convinced their children were on their way for a visit. At least, she assumed they were confused. It would be heartless to say you'd come by, then didn't.

"Hello. Nice evening."

"Lola, it's me."

It was Marcy. Instead of heading in, Lola dropped into a nearby rocker. For some reason, whoever decorated the home decided the front porch needed to be crowded with rockers. It was a cross between a Norman Rockwell photo and a Cracker Barrel store. All they needed was the oversized checkerboard.

"Did you decide you needed to stay out here and cry about your thoughtless lover?"

A derisive snort sounded. "I wanted to think about what we learned from Mabel while it's still fresh in my mind."

"I couldn't help noticing that Mabel called Sue Ellen by her first name, but Mr. Makowski was always *mister*."

"Hard to miss." Marcy rested her chin on her fisted hand. "What worries me is if that would make her unduly prejudiced."

"Didn't look like she had any trouble taking the financial settlement when he retired her."

Marcy dropped her hand and turned to catch Lola's eyes. "He let Mabel go fast enough. He held onto the house much longer. No way a businessman like him would be taking care of that big house on his own. We need to know why he let Mabel go."

"It was obvious she wasn't a fan of the man."

"True. You don't have to be a fan to get the job done. Most employees hate their bosses. If not hate, then a healthy disdain. Maybe, he felt she knew too much."

"Could be." She mulled over the possibility, feeling much more alive than she had a few minutes ago. "Mabel strikes me as a sharp knife. He might not want her around because she would notice too much."

"Excellent!" Marcy pushed her closed fist near Lola.

"Hey! Just because I thought of it first is no reason to get testy."

Laughter greeted the remark. "Oh, Lola, it's a fist bump. We touch closed fists lightly as a sign of self-congratulations. All the kids are doing it."

"The cool kids?"

"Most definitely."

Lola balled up her fist and tapped Marcy's still fisted hand. "I always was one of the cool kids."

Chapter Eleven

I T DIDN'T TAKE Herman long to discover all their efforts at secrecy were basically wasted. No matter where they met, Eunice would sniff it out. Their cold case group was already responsible for an upcoming dance and garden plots in the spring. They couldn't handle anything else. Marcy, the veteran detective, had suggested the solution. No surprise there. She decided not to have any secret meetings, but to meet by *accident,* usually in groups of two and converse normally. If anyone showed interest in their conversation, they would claim they were talking about a television show and they couldn't quite remember its name. It was a version of hiding in plain sight.

Muffled voices shouting in the distance caused Herman to glance at Marcy. The woman brought her wheelchair to a stop, which was a blessed relief for Herman. Every rotation of her wheels was like three of his steps. He was never one for speed walking. On top of that, Marcy managed to chat away without appearing the least bit winded.

The dining room door burst open as a white smocked dietary employee exited shaking his head. He spotted Herman and Marcy and held up his hand. "Don't go in there. Those people are crazy! Figure I'll head out for a break until they wind down."

Crazy people. Herman had a feeling he just might know a few of them. Marcy cut her head to the dining room door, signaling their destination. He held the door open. "I'll bet you five dollars Eunice is involved."

Marcy wheeled through, throwing back over her shoulder. "I don't take sucker bets."

A dozen or more residents marched around the dining room carrying signs. A few with walkers had the signs awkwardly pinned to their backs. They included the messages *I MAY BE OLD BUT I STILL CAN CHEW, WE WANT REAL FOOD, WHERE'S THE BEEF?* and *TASTE IS AN IMPORTANT SENSE, TOO.*

Gus and Eunice held a large banner between them, but it was hard to read since they seldom kept it taut. All he really could see was the word *DOGFOOD*. It was hard to know if they were comparing the food *to* dogfood or if they were asking for it as an alternative. Even more surprising was Gus working with Eunice. He couldn't stand her.

Herman's eyes roved over the crowd looking for Jake, who had originally mentioned his suspicions about the dietician shortchanging the residents. Not too surprisingly, he wasn't here. The man was smart enough to know when to show up and when to stay far, far away.

"Let's hear it." Eunice directed through an old-fashioned megaphone best remembered from old 1940s movies and football games. "We want food, we can chew, chew, chew!"

The group followed the chant with Delores, the retired opera singer, turning the last word into a solo that soared around the room. A hair-netted employee peeked out from behind a door, then withdrew her head in a hurry. Seniors revolting had to be a novel sight. If it were teachers, even students, the television news would be here filming.

He leaned closer to Marcy to be heard over the chanting. "Do you think the administration will do anything?"

"If they were that concerned, they'd be here already. Besides, I see one of the residents from the dementia unit, which means they'll play it off as a bunch of confused residents."

"Why judge the group by one or two people?"

Marcy shrugged. "People do it every day. There're over a million cops working in the United States, but the news only reports on about a dozen or more clearly inferior officers, and we're all painted with the same brush. That's the media for you. The old newspaper slogan was *if it bleeds, it leads* tells it all."

Eunice brandished her megaphone before placing it to her lips. "Call your congressman! Your senator!"

"That won't do any good." Marcy shook her head. "See if you can get the megaphone away from Eunice and bring it to me."

Really? Was she asking him to take on Eunice? He remembered what happened to his friend, Detective Tabor, and Officer Wells when they tried to remove the same rebel rouser from Legacy Beach. She threw pails of cold ocean water on them and had a surprisingly good aim. What kind of gentleman would he be if he failed to help a lady and a wounded first responder? How could he do this without getting hurt? A brilliant thought occurred to him as he hustled over to where Eunice stood and grabbed the megaphone when the woman put it down on a nearby table.

He put the megaphone to his lips. "Great turnout. Detective Marcella Collins wants to address the crowd." He figured if he used her full name it would convey more authority.

A sour look crossed Eunice's face. She narrowed her eyes and wrinkled her nose as if smelling a skunk nearby. "She's not going to tell us to disband and to go quietly to our rooms and watch the daytime game shows?"

"Oh, no!" He hoped she wouldn't, due to not having a clue. If Eunice didn't like what Marcy had to say, she'd take it out on him. He shuddered. No telling what the devious woman might do. By this time, he didn't want the megaphone. If there was any way he could walk out of the dining room on good terms with everyone, he wished it would miraculously take shape in his mind. *Nothing.* He was committed to carrying it to Marcy.

He handed over the cone, mentally praying he'd not regret his decision to be helpful.

Marcy cleared her throat and threw him a reassuring smile, then held it up to her mouth. "Ladies and Gentlemen, can I have your attention, please?" The marchers shuffled to a stop, recognizing the voice of authority. She allowed a significant pause before continuing. "Every one of you matters very much to someone. Call your children. Your grandchildren. Invite them to dinner. Let them see how bad the food is. Those of you with social media accounts, take photos of the food and post it. Do this daily with captions like 'Would you eat this?'"

The marchers nodded and broke into various discussions. Feeling buoyed by the outcome and a lack of retribution, Herman grabbed the megaphone. "We can start a petition. Call the newspaper." The ideas were flowing. Maybe he should have been a lobbyist. Before he could share another one, a sharp pain in his side caused him to glance down.

Eunice glared up at him and held out her hand. "My megaphone. Should have known you would try to steal the spotlight. Gus told me to watch out for you, that you were a glory hog."

"Gus!" Herman swiveled his head looking for the man. He almost missed him since Gus decided to sit. He marched over to his former friend, indignant that he would malign him so. He made sure to face the man where he could be sure he heard him. "You've been talking trash about me to Eunice?"

He raised his bushy eyebrows, then chuckled. "She sucked you in, didn't she?"

"What do you mean?"

"Whoo-wee!" Gus slapped his thigh. "If we had that gal spinning her yarns and causing chaos, the war would have been much shorter. She came to me and told me that Jake thought I didn't have the salt to head up a food rebellion, that he would be the natural leader."

"Aha, I see where this is going. Good chance Jake knows nothing about this." He chuckled. "Silly of me to be fooled by Eunice. I thought you called me a glory hog."

"Well, I did, and you are."

Herman opened and closed his mouth without saying anything. How could his friend accuse him of such a thing?

"Don't go getting your shorts in a wad. Most men are when alone with countless women. It's probably human nature. Everyone wants the story to be all about them. They want the credit. The starring role."

"Even you?"

"Of course. Why do you think I volunteered to be an explosives expert?"

His anger faded when he realized Gus had attributed him with a less than desirable characteristic that he figured most of the human population had, including himself. Putting it that way, it didn't sound too bad. "Okay. I was mad, but I'm over it." He put out his hand, and Gus shook it. "Friends?"

"Absolutely. At my age, I can't afford to lose any more friends. So, friend, how about a ride in your vehicle to get some food?"

"No can do. Can't take too many chances. I can go out and bring something back. We could eat in the courtyard area. The weather is pleasant."

"Woohoo, I can't wait!" Gus shouted, earning Eunice's attention.

The wiry woman pivoted and placed a hand on her hips as she regarded both men with a suspicious stare. "What can't you wait for?"

Gus took Eunice's hand and made a courtly bow. "I can't wait until we have dance night and the opportunity to dance with you."

Such a blatant lie shouldn't fool the woman, but Eunice flushed and pulled her hand back to wave in front of her face. "My goodness, Gus. I had no clue you cared."

It sounded like Herman's cue to leave. He came up behind Marcy and warned her. "We need to leave now, before we're associated in any manner with the explosion that's about to happen."

"What do you mean?" Marcy gave her chair a strong push to get it rolling. "People should be able to protest the food, especially when they don't have an alternative."

"Speaking of that. I'm heading out to grab a bucket of chicken. It's the least I can do with Gus taking a bullet for us."

"I don't understand, but whatever. Can I come along? I'd like to do a timed run of how long it would have taken Sue Ellen's husband to reach the house. You'll have to pick up your speed, too. Not enough to get a ticket, though."

"Didn't the former detective do that already? They always do that kind of stuff on television."

Marcy groaned. "Television. If only I had a dollar for every person who mentioned television to me while we were investigating a crime. No, we don't have all the cool equipment you see on television. Most television shows focus on one crime. It has been my experience that criminals don't wait for you to solve one crime before committing another. Often, I had more than one case on my desk at once. Some get more attention than others."

"Which ones?" Herman asked as he held the exterior door open.

"Duh. What do you think?"

On television, all crimes were important, even the murder of a homeless person. They all got solved in a timely, neat fashion. No need to mention that and have his head handed to him. "The ones with important folks involved in it."

"You'd think that. Those impressed with their own worth definitely put the pressure on us. However, the cases that get the most attention are the ones with the most clues and the best likelihood of being solved."

That made sense. "Okay. What about Sue Ellen's case? How would you classify that?"

"It was dismissed as a case when it was labeled suicide. Technically, it isn't truly a cold case, more of a sore spot for my former partner, Lance. It was one of those unsolvable cases."

Did she even listen to herself talk? "You think we can solve this when professionals shelved it?"

Marcy grinned, "We have something the regular police don't have."

"The combined intelligence of life experience of five seasoned individuals." He puffed as he considered that their shared years would be put to good use.

"I was thinking free time. We have hours and hours to consider what could have happened."

Herman jingled his keys as they approached his car. He never thought of having endless, unoccupied time as an attribute. Now he did.

Chapter Twelve

M ARCY HELD UP the notebook, pulling it a little bit back from her face to bring it into focus. The car wreck resulting from chasing a perp from a drive-by shooting not only crushed her leg, but also caused massive trauma to her head. If she hadn't called for backup, the thug would have polished her off. He shot wildly at her as she tried to shake off the powder fog from the exploded airbag. The powder particulates hanging in the air may have saved her, or it could be he was just a bad shot. Even at close range, she only got a bullet to the shoulder and another grazed her cheek.

Just when she thought she'd almost shaken off the incident and was mere steps from full recovery, something else showed up. Most people approaching fifty had diminishing vision. That was probably all it was. Many veteran officers and detectives wore glasses or contacts. It wasn't that big of a deal, but it bothered her. Every physical issue felt like a backward slide. Would she ever be well?

They had left the food protest in the dining room with hopes of retracing Todd Makowski's route to his house when notified of his wife's death.

"Have you figured out an address yet?" Herman asked from his position behind the wheel.

"He had an office on Pearl Street at the time. The man has since moved. We'll turn left on Green Valley and head toward State. We'll pick up the chicken on the way back. There's a chain restaurant not too far from the Makowski home."

The car growled to life. Herman put the sedan into drive and carefully maneuvered his way through the parking lot. Her first instinct was to tell him he could drive a little more than five miles an hour. After all, Herman could come and go like many of the retirees in the H wing of the center. Those in the A and B wings needed the most care. Gus was the first to figure out if he made the hike to H wing, he could leave without setting off any alarms. Most residents either didn't know this or were unwilling to make the hike. If nothing else, it would be good to know for future group forays.

"In the future, it might be to your benefit to park near H wing."

"Are you crazy?" He grimaced as he drove. "It's dangerous over there. All those senior citizens driving might hit my car."

"You're a senior citizen."

"I know." He nodded, then added, "A senior who can drive. I don't take it lightly. Always signal. Drive the speed limit."

"Under the speed limit." She glanced at the speedometer that hovered at a mere fifteen as opposed to the thirty that was posted.

"Complain, complain." The car increased in speed all the way up to twenty. "It always amazes me that when you drive folks around, all they do is tell you how to drive."

"That's the problem with people in general, having opinions that aren't the same as your own. At the next light, I need you to turn left."

"Got it. So, what's this reenactment supposed to prove, anyhow?"

That's the problem with reenactments. You usually had a premise you were trying to prove, but it didn't always work the way you wanted it to. Sometimes, it proved just the opposite, which stomped out any working premise she might have. It had happened to her more than once when she insisted on doing one. Even though they did it on the television all the time, in real life it was only used because there was nothing else left to do.

A flash of color caught her eye. On the side of the road, a woman was jogging. At one time, she'd be out running the trails. That had been more than a few years ago. The jogger kept pace with them as opposed to them pulling away. "Herman, did you slow down?"

"Yes. I'm coming to a stop sign. Figured you might want me to stop at it."

The was a large octangular sign a few meters ahead.

"Yes." No wonder Herman was so fussy about everyone telling him how to drive. If she'd paid attention instead of woolgathering about the past, she would have seen the sign. She waited until he stopped to answer his earlier question. "I hope by doing the reenactment we can see how long it would *reasonably* take to drive there."

"I noticed you emphasized reasonably there. What's up?" He braked for the stop and allowed the jogger to cross before starting up again.

"That's the thing with reenactments, you don't know what really happened. You're told one thing, not necessarily the truth, but it is all you have to go on. We'll drive the normal speed. Due to the one-way streets, there aren't that many ways to get from Pearl Street to the Makowski home."

Herman appeared to mull it over. "If I had ever married and I found out something happened to my wife, I would have been there in a heartbeat. Maybe the husband sped."

"Good reasoning. I thought the same. The husband would have to go through one of the most profitable speed traps in the area. It would be hard for him not to be caught. If he were stopped and explained the situation, he might get an escort or at least use it as an alibi for where he was."

The stoplight flashed red, causing the car to shudder to a stop. Herman took the opportunity to glance at Marcy and hoist an eyebrow. "No need for him to prove anything if it was suicide."

"True. I wasn't there and can only go by the notes. I do wonder if there was a moment when they considered the husband as the culprit, but I'm probably a little biased."

"You certainly are. Do you know the guy? Got something against him?"

A horn honked behind him, seconds after the light turned green. "Keep your pants on." He coasted through the light about as slow as he possibly could. To go any slower would involve them using their feet, like in those Flintstone cartoons. The light was even turning as they exited the intersection.

"Herman." She gave him a knowing look. "You did that on purpose."

"Maybe." He chuckled. "Bet that young whippersnapper won't be quick to honk again."

"Ha. I wish. He probably won't process the message you were trying to send him. Okay, we're almost there. Pull into the empty space in front of the building and park. My information is that his office is on the second floor. Let's pretend you get a call about your wife. Hello, Mr. Makowski? Something terrible has happened to your wife. Come home fast."

Herman shifted the car into drive, but Marcy placed a restraining hand on his arm. "Not yet. He has to get down the stairs. Let's wait five minutes." She held up her watch and waited for the second hand to make five sweeps. "Go!"

They drove through the route three times. Even with Marcy

making calculations for the husband driving faster, they never arrived anywhere close to the time Mabel said the husband arrived, which could only mean two things. The husband wasn't at work, or Mabel wasn't correct about the time.

Herman had been a good sport about the whole thing, but she still asked, "Want to try for a fourth time? I'm getting pretty good at the route."

"You are." He had even picked up speed on the last run. "We better go pick up the chicken. Even if Gus was willing to eat in the dining room, I bet after today's antics he wouldn't be welcomed."

"I don't know." Herman used one hand to steer the car over to the side of the street and parked. "I keep trying to put myself in the husband's shoes. Wouldn't he be frantic? Maybe he might have sped or even wrecked. All that would make sense. All I can tell from the notes is that he shows up and is coherent. Doesn't that seem a bit off to you?"

Sometimes being an officer of the law made her a little jaded when it came to her fellow citizens. The man sitting next to her had served in the war, lost friends, and yet he retained a certain naiveté she wished she still had. "Definitely. Doesn't mean he killed her. Things could not have been good between the two of them for a while. He said she was depressed. He could have been expecting this. He may have already moved on without the benefit of divorce."

"Interesting." His index finger tapped his temple. "We know Mabel was not a fan of the husband. If she knew some hanky-panky was going on, that would explain her attitude."

"We need to go." She pointed forward. "At the end of this street, turn left. We should get some sides, too."

"I agree. I got a feeling if we show up with real food, we'll have a lot more people than we originally expected."

With a slight lurch, the car shifted into drive and moved forward. She knew enough not to say anything. The man had pride. Sometimes, it was all people had left. The problem with the case was much of what they had was prejudiced by the people involved. She wasn't sure if Mabel or Todd Makowski had told the entire truth to the police. Nowadays, it had become a thing to speak your truth. What it really meant was *state an opinion*. Facts weren't usually involved in speaking their truth. They might have a case of two individuals speaking *their* truth, which wouldn't do Sue Ellen or her any good.

"Let's get a big bucket. We have a lot to discuss."

Herman spotted the restaurant and flipped on his turn signal. "I hope this isn't going to be on my dime. This case is costing me money, which is not something I agreed to."

His comment made her laugh. It reminded her of when she was a radio car cop and her partner was continuously griping about always paying for lunch. He didn't. "I got it, partner."

Chapter Thirteen

T HE AUTOMATIC DEODORANT sprayer hissed and spewed out a chemical concoction, supposed to be a floral garden, spring morning, or something near it, according to the aide she asked when she first arrived. Allegedly, it made the place feel homier. Lola confessed upon smelling that it didn't work, which made the aide chuckle. The cloying scent didn't cover up the smell of antiseptic wipes, floor cleaner, or some of the more unpleasant scents wafting from the full care units.

Whether the scents were better or worse than Vegas was hard to decide. The elegant Vegas she loved, with men in tuxedoes and women in evening dresses, had changed to folks in scooters with oxygen tanks playing the slots. The streets were crowded with people of different nationalities, many carrying or holding hands of their progeny while someone else's children attempted to get them to take stripper cards. Some of the vacationing children would pick up the cards only to have it snatched out of their hands by their mothers. Some of the hotels even catered to the families with circus or medieval shows.

No, it definitely wasn't the adult playground of her past. The homeless population had even invaded the strip. There had always been buskers who would dress up in crazy outfits and pose for a photo for tips, but now those opportunistic individuals had to compete with pathetic homeless people holding up homemade signs using words like *veteran* and *penniless*, which usually grabbed the loose change that would have gone to someone dressed up like a comic book character. No, nothing was the same. She told herself she moved here because *she* changed, but maybe it was Vegas that had.

At least here, if someone was sleeping in her doorway, she could call an orderly and have them hauled back to their right location. The final straw that had her agreeing to move was the second time she was mugged close to her home. Nothing matters if you don't feel safe. At least here, she felt secure, bored sometimes, but never threatened.

Lola clutched the tote bag she had shoved the paper plates, plastic forks, and napkins into. After Gus and Eunice's rally today, no extra service would be forthcoming from the dietary area. The dining room had been temporarily closed. The administration treated it like it was a punishment. For some, with it being the only social interaction they had all day, it was. Normally, she avoided the dining room since that made her realize she was in a nursing home. Instead, she liked to think she was in a third-rate hotel with other travelers.

The impromptu lunch was scheduled outside in the courtyard. They had talked about gardening, but only as a cover. It was too late in the season to do anything. The weedy grass with bare stretches of dirt and concrete benches didn't tempt too many outdoors, especially those in wheelchairs. To get through the two sets of doors to get outdoors was too much work.

Gus told her to pick up Jake on the way here. They agreed to only show up in twos, rather like animals wandering to the ark. Lately, Jake had been absent. It made her wonder what was going on. When she reached Jake's room on D ward, she gave a spritely knock.

"Room service."

"Just a minute."

Lola tapped her foot as she waited, counting silently under her breath. The scent of cookies and cream slipped under the door. Maybe Jake already had his own snacks and didn't really care if Herman was bringing back chicken.

The door swung open revealing Jake, dapper in a black shirt with a striped ascot.

"Snazzy. I appreciate a man who still cares about his appearance."

Jake smiled and held out his bent arm. "My lady, may I escort you to the al fresco dining?"

She took the proffered arm and imagined he was one of her many admirers when she was forty years younger, before releasing it to hold onto her walker. Realistically, most of her admirers only wanted to be seen with a leggy showgirl and probably saw the lot of them as interchangeable. It was nice when a man actually got your name right. She'd been called Liza, Luci, Lisa, and Lolly. Really? *Lolly*? When she corrected one of her admirers, whom she suspected was part of the Mafia, he shrugged and grunted *whatever*.

Lola took a side glance at her escort. Jake still carried himself well. His shoulders were back, and his head was up as if he imagined all eyes were on him. No wonder the ladies of Greener Pastures often sat waiting for him to pass by them and offered an airy compliment. He probably had the lot of them bringing him yummy treats. None they made themselves, but something they ordered online.

"Thought much about the case?"

"Some."

Two gossipy biddies to her left made her straighten up so she didn't look as old. She fixed Jake with a warm smile that had him grinning back. Take that! Lola still had it. The man pool might be limited at the center, but she still knew how to fish it or at least give the appearance of doing so. Not like she had her eye on Jake, but rather she wanted to honk off the fusspots. Just the other day she overheard them talking trash about her in Bingo. Saying things about her being a showgirl, they caught each other's eyes and laughed. It was a mean laugh. The kind you expected from the schoolyard bully after he tripped someone.

If she made one of them uncomfortable, thinking she'd caught Jake's eye, it would be sufficient payback. Of course, if nothing ever came of their relationship, they'd gossip about that, too.

When they were far enough away from being overheard, she spoke. "We're going to have to have a very public fight sometime soon. It will let the ladies know you're back on the market."

He chuckled. "I can do that. Anything we should argue about?"

"Don't care. It could even be television shows for all I care. The important thing is I have to throw you over."

"Got it. That always makes the women sympathetic. If I threw you over, the jealous ones would say you deserve it, but the decent ones would think I was the jerk. I've always had a weakness for the good girls."

"Yeah, most men do." She heaved a sigh. "They usually marry them."

The interior door to the courtyard opened, and Gus peeked around the corner. "Hurry up, you two."

Jake gestured to his friend. "We'll be there when we're there and not a second sooner."

The door closed behind Gus as he retreated to the courtyard. They'd talk about the case with their impromptu dinner party unless

Eunice was present. She could turn up due to the woman's superior sleuthing skills.

She'd sidled up to Lola during therapy-dog session and pointed out which staff member was getting divorced, which one snuck out for a cigarette every chance she could, and who started Weight Watchers but was stealing calorie-rich treats from the staff refrigerator. The administration assumed it was a resident as opposed to a staff member. All the information turned out to be true, which meant a person had to be very careful around Eunice.

"You never mentioned what you thought about the case."

Jake cleared his throat and stopped his progress to the door. "I know Marcy wants to solve this case, but what if there is nothing to solve? Occam's Razor states that the simplest solution or answer is usually the correct one."

"Maybe, but what if it isn't true?"

His shoulders went up into a shrug, then he went to the door and held it open for her. "I guess we'll have to see what the others have to say."

Chapter Fourteen

THE CONCRETE BENCH could easily earn the title as the most uncomfortable seat ever. Marcy shifted, trying to find a comfier position. There was none. The wheelchair might be a better choice, but she refused to go back to it until the meeting was over. If her goal was to return back to her old job solving crimes, she wasn't going to do it from a wheelchair.

Plenty of cops carried extra pounds, which caused an occasional lecture at the yearly checkup or review. What there wasn't was any cops with obvious handicaps. No blind, no deaf, no cops in wheelchairs due to the perception that it would hamper them doing their duty. She'd worked with her share of racist, sexist, and just plain lazy individuals. If offered an intelligent, hard-working individual with wheels over one of the doofuses she'd endured previously, she'd take the wheelchair person in a heartbeat. The problem was, she wasn't in charge of hiring.

Truth was, when it came to a chase the cop in the wheelchair was at a serious disadvantage. No one would take her seriously until she gave up the chair. Even then, there would be talk about how frail she was and how she might get hurt. They'd call her a liability and worry that she might sue the department or some other nonsense. After her accident and before her surgery, some HR person was shoving some waiver at her to sign. It waived her right to sue for injuries that occurred on the job. A lawyer friend informed her that the waiver wouldn't stand up in court. She had signed it while medicated for the upcoming surgery. It could also be argued that she was coerced into signing.

The exterior door swung open admitting Lola and Jake. About time. She wasn't going to resort to sharing a communal container of coleslaw or mashed potatoes. Lola had promised to bring the dishes. She settled for a wave, but Gus wasn't nearly as reticent.

"Get a move on." He hopped down from the ornamental boulder he was standing on and hurried over to greet the newcomers. He put his hand to his head as if doffing a hat in Lola's direction. "I was talking to Jake, not you. You can take as long as you want."

She giggled and held out a tote bag to Gus. "The plates and forks are in there. Along with some napkins."

Soon the men were all crowding around the food, making contented noises. Lola took a seat beside Marcy.

"I have to warn you this bench is not exactly memory foam. It does not conform to your dimensions."

There was a twinkle in Lola's faded blue eyes as she replied. "It is what it is. I imagine when we start that big remodel of the garden, the center will order us furniture."

"It depends. I would have said no, but it could be a feature that would appeal to potential residents or more likely to their families."

Jake and Herman carried two plates and offered one to Marcy and the other to Lola. "Ah, gentlemen, thank you. You are a rare and vanishing breed."

Marcy shook her head, considering the total dearth of gentlemen in her life. "Ain't that the truth. Gather around team. We'll have to talk fast, because I can't guarantee how long it will be before real food is sniffed out."

Gus moved closer to his plate and waved his fork for emphasis.

"Don't forget about Eunice."

Herman sighed. "As if we could."

With her plate precariously balanced on her legs, she clapped her hands. "No time for that. We need to report. Herman, you can report on our little crime reenactment today."

"You got to do a crime reenactment and didn't invite me?" Gus's bushy eyebrows shot up, announcing his indignation.

Before Herman could say anything, Marcy did. "You were busy having your food protest. Besides, I have a suspicion you might have some information for me."

He gave her a broad wink and saluted. "Right you are, Captain." He gestured to Herman. "Age before brilliance."

"Age before brilliance, my foot." Herman glared at Gus, then laughed, proving his irritation was feigned. "We ran the route from the office to the house three times. There wasn't much variation because of the one-way streets. No matter which way the man drove, he would still have to go through that notorious speed trap near the railroad tracks where the city earns most of its ticket revenue. If he was speeding, he would have been stopped, and there is no mention of it. If the husband was going an appropriate speed, he could never have made it to the house in the time Mabel said he did."

"Okay," Jake held up his hand. "The police say Makowski arrived in under ten minutes. What is this time based on?"

Marcy had originally thought they were taking Mabel's word for how long it took for the husband to arrive, which would be a subjective guess at best. "On the way back here, I called Lance to see how they computed the time. Mabel called the husband first, then 911. It was computed from the time of the 911 call to the man's appearance. He showed up shortly after the squad car."

"Makes me wonder," Gus took a hefty bite of chicken and

chewed, keeping the others speculating about what he might be thinking about, "if the man was somewhere he shouldn't be. Why else lie about it?"

"Girlfriend?" Herman suggested as he lifted a forkful of mashed potatoes to his lips. He inhaled the potatoes, then continued. "Why not get a divorce? Plenty of people are doing it. I heard on one of those trivia shows it was about fifty percent."

"It's not their way," Lola added from her perch on the bench. "Now, I may not be related to rich folks, but I have come in contact with plenty. Money marries money. I've seen and heard of women putting up with neglect, cheating, even abuse to maintain their affluent lifestyle. If there's money, there's prenups, too. It would be interesting to know who had the money in the family. Were there any prenups? Pay-out on life insurance?"

"Good call." Marcy nudged the woman. "The team is coming together. Prenups are usually confidential, but that confidentiality probably doesn't extend past death. Even so, there are plenty of people who might know, including Mabel. As I mentioned before, both husband and wife had money. An insurance pay-off should be easy enough to find out. It wasn't confidentiality protected. Lance even looked into it when he was considering the husband as a possible suspect. He gave it up when they shut the case down."

"Doesn't seem right." Lola brought her closed hand to her face. "Was there no one to plead Sue Ellen's case?"

It had seemed that way to her, too. Marcy sighed heavily. "I guess Lance kinda felt that way. Her parents had died a few years ago in a tragic plane crash. Her father was piloting the small jet and missed the runway in the fog. With no siblings, Sue Ellen inherited the bulk of the fortune."

Jake whistled. "Until now, I figured it was a suicide. It seemed like the simplest explanation. Money can cause people to do stupid things."

"When we were driving, didn't you say the parents died a few years before she did?" Herman asked, as he helped himself to more chicken."

"I did." Marcy concurred. "If you're thinking the husband couldn't be guilty because he would have killed her right away, take into consideration how big estates are in probate a long time. It takes a while to value the assets and liquify them for distribution. Not sure when the final payout happened. What we do know is Sue Ellen changed her will before her death without her husband's presence."

"Hmm…" Lola lengthened the word and arched her eyebrows. "Makes me think she knew something was going on. You said something before about the husband not being in the will. Basically, she spent the bulk of her money on homeless kittens and puppies. The love was definitely gone. I'm thinking she might have expected something to happen to her. That's why she changed her will."

"Could be." It was an angle she hadn't even considered yet. Marcy wanted to be a hundred percent sure it wasn't suicide, first. Calling something murder didn't necessarily make it so. "It makes me think she would have left a letter or something behind. There was talk about a note, but nothing concrete. No copy or photo, which makes me wonder if there was one at all."

Gus moved a little closer to Marcy. When he was about a foot from her, he waved his arms. "It's my turn! We don't have all day."

Instead of speaking, she shot out her index finger and thumb as if a gun. Gus must have thought it was a starting pistol because he started talking. "Most of you may not know that I have a laptop and am hooked up to the World Wide Web. That allows me to surf."

Jake wrinkled his nose. "Spare us the details of your late-night web searches."

"Truthfully…" Gus began, "…late night is best. There are fewer people looking up cute cat videos and stalking their relatives on social media. I assume there are fewer people strolling through public records, too."

"Can you cut to the chase?" Herman suggested, with a glance back to the interior door.

"Sure." Gus bobbed his head in agreement. "The husband stayed in the house until it sold. He put it on the market right away, but it didn't sell for a year since no one wants to live in a house where someone offed themselves."

"Okay." Marcy gave him an encouraging smile and hoped he knew more than houses where people died in were harder to unload.

"He stayed in his Pearl Street business a little longer. He did move across the river to Louisville, Kentucky."

"No biggie." Jake interjected, then nodded to his friend, "Got anything a little meatier?"

Gus held up his hand. "How about he married his administrative assistant a few months after the suicide. Her name is Jill Olsen."

Marcy sat up a little straighter. "This is news."

"I bet she's some young blonde," Jake added with a smirk.

"You'd be wrong." Gus unfolded a piece of paper. "This is a picture taken when Makowski got some type of business award. Jill is in the left corner."

This was more than Lance had dug up, but the man had other things to do than to investigate a case that had been declared a non-case. Marcy squirmed as the three men stared at the photo. Herman had on his glasses but ended up passing them around to his two buddies for them to stare at the photo, too. They gave each other baffled looks before passing the picture to her and Lola.

Front and center was a middle-aged man with a receding hairline and the start of a double chin. He held some huge trophy that would probably equal the Super Bowl trophy in both size and weight. The verbiage underneath mentioned the other members of his team, including Jill Olsen on the left. The people in the background weren't all that clear. What she could pick out was a conservatively dressed woman with her hair pulled back and glasses.

Lola tapped her lacquered nail on the photo. "With the right makeup and clothes, she could be beautiful."

Herman snorted his disbelief. "You think?"

"I know." Lola crossed her arms. "You men see some fashion model or movie star, and you think the woman looks like that all the time. They usually have a dozen people to bring them up to that standard of beauty, then they enhance the image with digital magic. It's no wonder celebrities can go to the grocery store and not be recognized. They don't even look like their images."

The sound of people passing in the hallway corridor drifted into the courtyard. All it would take was a turn of the head for someone to see them. Once they saw them, they'd investigate—the staff, because it was their job, or curiosity would propel the residents outdoors.

"All right, folks," Marcy held her hands up for attention. "Let's recap. Sue Ellen died a wealthy woman. Her husband was not in the will."

"It doesn't mean there wasn't a life insurance policy," Gus shouted, proving he was indeed listening.

"I'll look into that. Makowski sold his house and moved his business to Louisville, possibly to escape any censure he might get for marrying soon after his wife's suicide. He married his personal assistant. He wasn't at work when Mabel called."

"Could have been nearby in his love nest with Jill," Lola added with a tap of her index finger to her temple. "It might be close to the house. Can you imagine a man bold enough to keep his mistress and wife that close together?"

Jake examined his nails while Herman looked at the ground to avoid answering. The men's attempt not to answer almost made Marcy laugh. Gus, on the other hand, seemed to be pondering the question.

"That must be why he was such a good businessman. He had to make every minute count."

Chapter Fifteen

THE BROCHURE THAT had convinced Lola to relocate to the home featured many activities in several different rooms. There were images of smiling seniors playing croquet, another with them playing cards, and a third with one of the attractive seniors reading in the library. Foolishly, she assumed the people in the photos were residents. She wasted a good month searching for the one who looked like Lorne Greene, the father on the *Bonanza* show. Her second search was for wherever the shots were taken. Finally, she conceded they, too, were stock photos.

Most of the activities took place in the Florida room, which meant they couldn't have other activities at the same time. It didn't matter if you didn't care for Miss Perry's Prancing Poodles. That was all that there was. Even the library, which consisted of donated books, many with their covers ripped off, was only a corner of the Florida room. A local bookstore donated books once a month. Lola learned the hard way you had to be quick to grab a romance. Those went fast, and they were never returned for someone else to read.

The activity director must have assumed the residents would actually read the instructions in small font next to the bookcase. Lola had to use her magnifying class to discover each book was supposed to be borrowed for two weeks. With no checkout, there was no way of knowing who had what. In the end, it probably didn't matter due to being donated books. Every now and then a staff member would donate something. Usually nothing useful, like the 1968 World Book collection that sat in the corner gathering dust. Whoever unloaded that gem probably took the full tax value of something you couldn't even give away at a yard sale.

The box of new books sat on a table. Whoever brought them in knew better than to shelf them. By the end of the day, the box would be picked clean. The battered books on the shelves were the rejects, books so uninteresting that residents in a home would pass them over. Dated technical manuals. Really? A twenty-six-volume set of woodworking plans, which begged the question if any of them would be allowed power saws. She picked up a coverless book and flipped it over to read the back. With a cover, she had a fighting chance of guessing what the book was about, as opposed to reading about it. She could hear footsteps and voices.

Her attempts at getting here before everyone else would be short-lived. They'd come in, grab all the books, not even bothering to read the back covers, and cart them back to their rooms where they'd hoard them. Lola shoved the book in her hand into the bag attached to her walker, then she shoved in another two books, hoping at least one would be decent. No one wanted any self-help or improvement books. Most people came to a point where they no longer wanted to improve themselves, but rather enjoy what time they had left without struggling every day to be something they were not.

She had her hand on a fourth book, deciding if she should take it.

"What are you doing?"

Startled, Lola dropped the book and turned slowly. Marcy winked at her. "I see you got here before the book junkies. Find anything good?"

"I'm not sure. Haven't had time to even read the first page. You got to be fast around here if you want any new books."

"About that. We might not have much time for reading. There's been a development in the case. We'll meet back in the courtyard. No one seems to use that place. I'm surprised the smokers don't use it."

"They have cameras on it."

"How do you know that?"

It felt good to know something someone else didn't for a change. Most of the time she felt like she was playing a game of catch-up. Not that the information would help their case, but it was good knowing something. "When I first moved here, it turned out a couple of staff members used the courtyard as their assignation spot. As you know, there are windows surrounding the courtyard. One day, the director was strolling the halls like a king checking out his kingdom when he noticed residents avidly staring out the courtyard windows. Once he discovered what had entranced a number of residents, he went ballistic. Fired the employees, then put up the cameras."

Marcy pursed her lips. "Normally, closed circuit cameras don't pick up sound or if they do, not all that well."

"No worries. They're attached to the building. Not sure if they're even on now. It's been a few years since the incident." She inserted the fourth book into her bag, which would make the walker a trifle heavy. "Who do you want me to get for our emergency confab?"

"Get Jake. He's closer to your unit. I'll go find Herman, who will get Gus. We'll meet ASAP. No lollygagging. This is an important development."

"Got it." Lola turned and aimed her walker to the door. As she entered the hall, she passed a gaggle of residents heading for the

Florida room at a fast pace. Skipping breakfast had paid off. Her original plan was to get some nibbles after her book finding mission, but now she would have to delay that, too.

★

THE FIVE OF them clumped around the two concrete benches. Gus wanted to climb the nearby boulder, but Marcy told him he had to stand near to hear, because she was not going to shout their information.

Herman rubbed his hands together and a sparkle showed in his eyes. "What's the new development?"

The four of them stared intently at Marcy, who cleared her throat. "Todd Makowski has just filed paperwork to emigrate. Lance called me this morning. Apparently, he thought this might happen and had an alert for when it did."

Jake and Herman exchanged concerned looks, while Gus asked, "Where to?"

"Ireland."

"Heard good things about it. Very green, plenty of pubs, and they still like Americans there." He crossed his arms as if that signaled the end of the conversation.

Obviously, a possible suspect leaving the country wasn't a good deal, but wouldn't he still have to pay if charged? Lola knew this wasn't her area of expertise, but she did hear things. "Murder has no statute of limitations."

"True." Marcy agreed, then grimaced. "The problem is extradition. Ireland and the US have friendly enough relations, so it might be possible to extract a high-profile individual but not someone who changes his name, possibly even his appearance. For all we know, Makowski will have an Irish accent, too, or a backstory that has nothing to do with his current life."

"This is assuming he's guilty." Jake sniffed, assuming a superior air as if he knew something they didn't. "A man can emigrate if he wants to. Might be he wants to retire to someplace more restful."

Marcy held up her hand with two fingers extended. "Two major issues with that theory. The first being his development of shell companies in Ireland. None bear his or his company's name. Obviously, he intends to move some money through them. The second is someone told him that the case was being reopened."

Oh, that was not good with only one person Lola could think of. "Mabel."

"I suspect it was her, too." Marcy beamed at Lola with approval.

Herman clapped his hands together two times. "Well then, if he moves it's practically an admission of guilt."

"Not quite." Marcy shook her head. "We need something to connect him to the death. Once Lance got the call the case was a suicide, most of the evidence was dumped. Instinct had him snagging the notes and photos."

They threw out suggestions. Herman, first.

"He wasn't at his office at the time of his wife's death."

Marcy sucked in her lips before answering. "Not being where you said you were isn't a crime. We have no eyewitnesses that he was or was not at the office. Then again, he didn't need to produce any since it wasn't deemed a homicide."

"The man wasn't cut up about his wife's death." Gus pointed out. "Married again as soon as possible."

Jake fielded that question. "Men, especially older men, marry when a spouse dies since they are used to being taken care of."

"Not buying it." One of Marcy's well-defined brows lifted. "That might be true for a man of modest means. Makowski could hire a housekeeper, cook, or anyone he needed to do something. The fact he married someone he had worked with for a number of years could mean they were already involved."

Gus interrupted her. "A good reason to kill the wife."

Marcy held her hand up. "Yes, we discussed this as a motive. Even though Makowski was not in his wife's will, I've discovered she had a hefty life insurance policy with her husband as the beneficiary."

"What use would that be?" Jake wrinkled his nose as if the answer were self-evident. "Insurance companies don't pay for suicides."

"They didn't use to." Lola smiled, not because she was in favor of suicide, but she knew something Jake didn't. It would do him good to lose that superior, cosmopolitan air. "Now, most have a two-year policy. I know because suicide isn't all that rare in Vegas, especially with plenty of people gambling away all they own on the drop of a card. The policy has to be carried for at least two years before the suicide happens."

"I thought of that, too." Marcy gave a slight nod. "We have to come up with something."

Gus waved his hand instead of blurting out as usual. "Why don't we go visit Mabel again?"

"Yeah," Herman agreed.

Jake appeared uncommitted. Finally, he cleared his throat and spoke. "Do you have the photos with you?"

Instead of replying, Marcy dipped her hand into the messenger bag she had slung across her body and handed the photos to Jake, who perused them.

"Do you know if Sue Ellen was right or left handed?"

Her brow wrinkled as she considered the matter. "I'm not sure.

That wasn't in the notes. I assume she was right-handed as ninety percent of the population is." Marcy pushed her bangs back behind her ear as her teeth worried her bottom lip. "No. Wait. She wasn't right-handed." She held up her left hand and flourished it. "I'm left-handed. I remember my mother commenting that I wasn't the only left-handed woman in town after she'd seen Sue Ellen at a fundraiser."

Jake handed back the photo. "This woman was shot on the right side at close range. It wouldn't be impossible to do it with your left hand, but the angle would be awkward with more than a possibility of missing. Why would a left-handed person even attempt to commit suicide by using their non-dominant hand?"

Oh, that was a good question. Lola wished she would have thought of it herself. "Don't forget the jewelry, especially the big blue diamond. No one has tried to sell it."

"Lance put out alerts if anyone tried to do so. No one has so far."

"It was missing from the photo, and her hands were intact. The ring might be a connection, too."

Gus held up his left hand and stared at it. "How weird that all the clues focus on the left hand."

"Well, gang, we got some research to do, people to talk to, and a field trip in our near future," Marcy announced, keeping her countenance stern. She pointed to Gus, "I need you to do some research for me ASAP."

He waved his hands back and forth. "No can do." He checked his watch. "Eunice and I are meeting with the press in about ten minutes. I better get going if I want to reach the lobby in time. We agreed to meet them outside to keep the administration from silencing our voices about the state of our diet."

"I'll help." Jake raised his hand. "My niece, Katie, works in accounting. There's been an empty cubicle in her office after they let the other bookkeeper go. She lets me come in and use the desk computer. I might even be able to print out some stuff."

"Good." Marcy smiled at the man. "Your assignment is Jill Olsen, now Makowski. The more current the information and photo, the better. Keep your eye out for a sizable diamond."

Asking a man who wasn't a jeweler to look for diamonds just seemed wrong. Lola might not own any rings with six-figure price tags, but she had looked at plenty. A girl could dream. "I'll help."

Gus moved toward the door. He stopped and glanced back. "See if you can get a peek at what's being allotted for food."

Marcy closed her eyes and winced, while Lola peered into the corner where she knew the security camera was. There was no blinking red light. "I don't think it's on."

"Good. Okay, team, you have your orders. Herman and I are going on a trip to see Mabel." She held up her hand to halt any possible complaints. "It will probably be a fruitless trip. It's starting to look like Mabel was better friends with Mr. Makowski than Mrs. Makowski. She probably won't even answer the door since she just alerted the man."

Lola didn't want to leave without feeling like she had contributed to the discussion. "Maybe. Could be she was attached more to the money than the people who went with it. Makowski could have been told by someone else, too."

Marcy shot both hands through her hair. "I thought that, too. I couldn't come up with anyone."

This was her one chance to shine. The only thing she had over her fellow teammates was she'd experienced a great deal of human nature, mainly the dark side that people tried to hide. It was not surprising that people had come up with the expression *What happens in Vegas, stays in Vegas.* Someone had something to gain by stopping the investigation. "Who put the kibosh on the investigation?"

Marcy looked thoughtful for a few moments. "That would have been the former Police Chief Emmett Watson."

Chapter Sixteen

MARCY AND HERMAN headed out to the parking lot a little after ten and about twenty minutes later than they planned to. A young employee dogged their steps.

"Are you sure you're supposed to be leaving?"

It was the same conversation they'd endured for a while. The earnest young man, whose name tag read Ray, was intent on stopping them. Thank goodness he didn't try to manhandle either of them. Marcy might be in a chair, but she probably still had some moves to put a hurting on him. At this rate, the fellow would be running beside the car.

"Ray, you look like a smart guy."

This smoothed out the young staffer's furrowed brow a little. Herman continued strolling toward the car as he talked. "I realize you're new here. They probably told you there were all sorts of levels of people staying here, right?"

He nodded, but maintained a slight look of panic, while checking out the area to possibly see if there were any other employees he could recruit for backup. "Yeah."

"Good, good." Herman shot him his best trustworthy smile. "Some of us chose to come here. I'm retired and wanted to be around some folks my age. I'm able to come and go as I please." He rattled his car keys. "I wouldn't have these or a car if I wasn't."

Herman pressed on the fob to make his nearby car honk, which appeared to satisfy Ray. "Okay, obviously you do have a car. Why didn't you park closer to H wing, then?"

"It was full. There must have been a birthday party or something." He shrugged, but mentally reminded himself to park in H to avoid any future confrontations.

Finished with Herman, Ray turned his attention to Marcy, who glared at him and snarled, "Don't even start with me."

"Okay." He held his hands up and backed up slowly. "No need to get violent."

Herman hoisted a shaggy brow in Marcy's direction. "Remind me never to make you mad. Is that the face you show to your perps?"

A chuckle served as an answer as she rolled closer. "Oh no, that was my good cop façade."

"Yeah, I saw how reassured Ray was." They were almost to the car. No reason not to unlock or pop the trunk. He hadn't worked out how he was going to get Marcy in and out of the car. Last time, Jake handled it while he sat behind the wheel trying to monitor Gus, who was worse than a toddler sometimes. It was obvious he was the youngest of the three of them.

The last thing he wanted was to get on the wrong side of Marcy. He had the feeling she'd make Eunice look like a walk in the park.

"Will you stop looking at me as if I'm a rattlesnake? I'm not going to bite you. I'll wheel up to the trunk, then use the car as a support to work my way to the front seat. I'll be riding shotgun, of course."

Within a few minutes, they were on the road heading toward Mabel's house. Herman had his eyes glued to the unfamiliar road, sure a scooter or school bus would pull out in front of him. It certainly wasn't Legacy. There was a bit more traffic on the New

Albany streets than he was used to. Even back in Legacy, he hadn't driven that much. Only to get groceries or to treat himself to dinner. Usually, he just walked across the street to the inn where Donna would fix him something. He could call Donna and Mark. They'd certainly be a big help.

"Would it be okay if I called friends for help on the case?"

Marcy's head snapped up suddenly. She ignored the phone in her hand and fixed Herman with such a hot stare, he swore holes were being burned into his skin.

"It was just a suggestion." He did his best to backpedal. "No, it was a joke."

Marcy heaved a heavy sigh. "The short answer is no. Technically, I probably shouldn't have included all of you, but quite frankly, I wanted all the help I could get. The blow to the head scrambled things more than I like to admit. Look, Jake got the left-hand thing. Even a rookie would have gotten that, but I didn't. I'm betting I'll get back to a hundred percent, but part of me worries I might not. That's why I'm testy. I don't mean to be. I just keep thinking what if this is *it*? What if I'm in a chair forever or a mental fog settles over me when I think too long?"

"Most people do think something similar, even those who have never had anything bad happen to them—yet. I have faith that you'll get it all back. You are one determined lady."

"Yeah, I am." Marcy sat stiffly in her seat looking straight ahead. She spoke in a much lower voice. "What if I don't?"

Was she talking to him? Maybe not. Still, it would be rude to say nothing. As a lifelong bachelor, he didn't have much experience in reassuring women. What would he say to someone like Tennyson, his college-aged neighbor from Legacy? He'd be direct and honest.

"Deal with it as it comes. Don't go borrowing trouble. My granny used to say worry was like a runaway horse coming toward you that you spot from far away. You could fret about it, but the horse will run out of energy and never ever even make it to you." They came to a stoplight turning red, so he turned slightly to wink. "Guess you could update it and say trouble is like an Oldsmobile."

"They don't make those anymore."

"Figures. I think you get the gist."

"Yeah, I do." She reached over and patted him on the shoulder. "You're a nice guy. You would have made a great father and an even better grandfather."

"Maybe."

He turned away to stare out the windshield. The light flashed green. No way was he going to linger a second longer and have someone honk at him. He'd seen plenty of people in their cars, eating, drinking, or texting so they were slow to notice the light had changed. When they lingered at a light it was no big deal. If he did it, he was an old fogey or whatever people called elderly folks who were out of step with current society.

He didn't like to consider if he would have been a good husband or dad. He always thought he had time until he didn't. Sixty was the turning point for him. He wasn't some celebrity who could marry some young chick in an effort to accomplish what he had missed when he was younger. No, thank you. Wouldn't be fair to the woman or to the kid. If it could happen, which he doubted, everyone would be confused, thinking his son was his grandson or worse, great-grandson.

"Herman, what's got you looking all down?"

He hadn't realized he looked any way. "Nothing really. Maybe I was thinking about the road not taken."

"Hear ya. Everyone does that. In turn, they glamorize the road

117

not taken like it would have been much better. It wouldn't have. When you really want something, you find a way to get it, no matter what. The fact you haven't taken that road means you probably didn't want to take it."

"Thank you, Dr. Marcy. What do I owe you?"

"This time it's free. However, for future reference, I charge two hundred an hour."

Herman whistled. "Looks like I'll to have to solve my problems on my own."

"As I'm sure you will. Street's coming up. Turn left on Oak."

He followed the directions and was rather proud he had come this far relying just on memory. The old gray matter hadn't failed him yet. "I remembered," he felt compelled to mention, just to let Marcy know that he was as sharp as ever.

"I know. I tend to tell people what to do even when they know what to do. As you can imagine, I irritated most of my partners, until they realized that was one of my idiosyncrasies and it didn't reflect on them."

"I'd still find it irritating."

"Noted." She pointed to a dark sedan in front of Mabel's house. "I see Lance is here."

Lance? Herman knew he was the detective who handed the cold case to Marcy, but no one mentioned they were meeting him. "Should I be here if you're meeting Lance?"

"Please. The man understands I couldn't drive myself."

"Does he know how involved I am in the case?"

"No and I'd like to keep it that way. If you can get my wheelchair out, I'll roll over to meet Lance on my own."

"Mabel?" He hadn't exactly charmed the woman like Jake, but he thought he made a better impression than Gus, who camped out in the bathroom to search through her cabinets.

She shook her head. "I doubt there is a Mabel if she is the one who alerted Makowski. If she isn't, and he finds out she talked to us, it still seems like a safe bet to leave town."

"You, ah…" He paused, not wanting to put the possibility into words. "You don't think something bad has happened to her."

"That would be stupid. Makowski wants to emigrate. The last thing he would do is something that would leave him locked up behind bars in this country." The poodle lady had left her house and was walking slowly down the sidewalk. "Hey, I got an idea. You can go undercover."

"I'm afraid to ask." He was fairly sure it had something to do with the poodle lady.

"You saw the woman who just walked by?"

"Yep."

"Looks like she's your age. Strike up a conversation. Tell her you're interested in the neighborhood. Ask if Mabel's house might be on the market. That should get her talking. You could throw in a compliment or two. People tend to be more helpful to those they like. A nice-looking man like yourself should have no issues getting her to tell all she knows."

His hand went up to his hair and smoothed his thick, silver crown before getting out of the car. Once Marcy was situated and took off across the street, it was his turn. All he had to do was channel his smooth, international playboy persona. He stood there trying to decide on the proper approach for meeting the woman. Television taught him if the woman had a friend, he should spend his time talking to the friend instead. No friend here, unless he wanted to talk to the dog. That might work.

"What an adorable dog!" Herman called out as he crossed the

street. "Reminds me of my beloved…" he hesitated, trying to think of an appropriate dog name, "Lassie."

The woman looked up at his approach, but her expression wasn't exactly what he would label as welcoming. "With an unoriginal name like that, I'm sure your dog ran away."

That was hateful, but he managed a sad smile thinking about his imaginary dog. "Oh no, she was a faithful pet. Lived to be twenty-two. The vet said it was because I took extraordinary care of her."

She reached down to pet her dog. "Bet that dog was spoiled. Not like my Thor, here."

It was probably time for him to say something, but it was hard for Herman not to stare. The poodle and its owner had the exact same color of silver hair. Did she dye her hair to be the same as the dog? Did she buy the dog because it matched her hair? Did people do that? He was supposed to compliment her. "I bet you take excellent care of Thor."

She straightened and narrowed her eyes. "I do. If you think you're going to sell me some overpriced dog bed, you are sadly mistaken. Thor sleeps right beside me. I even embroidered his name on the pillowcase where he rests his head."

"That's nice." Creepy, if you asked him, but sometimes the truth was best left unsaid, especially for his purposes. "Nice neighborhood, too."

"What are you, a realtor?"

"No. Just interested in moving into a quiet neighborhood. I noticed most of the homes are patio homes. I like the idea of not having to go upstairs."

"Me, too. I suspect at your age, no one will give you a loan. Can't count on you living long enough to pay it off."

That was a kick in the teeth. Just goes to show not all little old ladies were sweet, grandmotherly types, but he knew that already. "No worries, I plan to pay cash."

"Oh, really." Her voice brightened as did her face. "I'm Amelia—just like the famous pilot. I like to think we both came from the same adventurous stock."

Greedy must be the word you're looking for, not adventurous. He held onto his smile as she tucked her free arm into his.

"So nice of you to escort me. A girl can't be too careful."

An opening—just what he needed. "Do you mean it's not a safe neighborhood?"

The lips pursed as her mind possibly raced on how to undo any deterrent she may have placed in the path of getting a man with money into the neighborhood. She patted his hand. "Mercy, no. It's a quiet place. Still, it can be lonely when it's only you. Are you a widower?"

"No." He realized he'd lost control of the conversation. Marcy and Lance were on the porch, talking, which had to mean Mabel was not home or not answering the door. "I'm a bachelor. Had a sweetheart, but by the time I got back from the war she'd moved on."

"How tragic…" Amelia cooed and took the opportunity to squeeze his hand.

The woman had a grip like a raptor. He might never get loose. Back to the business at hand, he gestured to Mabel's house. "My realtor is the one in the wheelchair. Not sure who the guy is. Anyhow, we were checking out if that house was available."

"Possibly. The owner is an odd sort. Sometimes, I can't sleep. Last night was one of those nights. I peered out the window, and there was Mabel stuffing her car with suitcases and whatnots. Odd time to pack for a vacation and an even odder time to move.

Furniture is still in the house. I checked."

"Strange. Could be she's moving across country, and it's cheaper to buy new stuff once she gets there." He had the necessary info. Now he needed to extract himself somehow. Marcy worked her way down the walk, and Lance held open the gate for her. He'd forgotten about the gate, but Marcy hadn't wanted him to go up the walk with her. "Oh, look, my realtor is done. We have some other locations to check."

Amelia's face fell a little. "Oh, really. Keep this place in mind. It's the safest. The folks on the corner are going to sell soon. They have two kids, and she's expecting a third. Check back in about a month, and I'm sure they'll have the for sale sign up." She gave his hand another squeeze. "You could just check back if you want to, even if the house isn't up for sale."

"Oh, all right. I'll do that. Got to go. Got to help Marcy into the car."

She released his hand, "It's noble of you to employ one of the disadvantaged."

Not knowing how to respond to that remark, he nodded his head, took a sidestep to be out of grabbing range and bumped into her poodle. Instead of whimpering or looking pathetic, it growled and snapped at his pants. His failure to keep current with fashion meant the trouser fabric wasn't even close to his leg.

"Stop that, Thor!" She waved a hand at the small dog until he released his grip. "I guess he felt dominated by your sheer height. He's always been the alpha male around the house."

"Uh, yeah, right." Alpha male? Dominate? The world had clearly moved on without him and did not send updates like his computer company did. He waved and made it across the street the same time Marcy reached the car.

Herman helped her into the car, then loaded the chair, feeling Amelia's eyes on him. He wasn't sure if she was evaluating him, his car, or possibly both. He got behind the wheel and exited the neighborhood without a word. When he reached the main drag, he released a heavy sigh.

"Sweet Jesus, I had serious doubts back there. I may have not done that much during the war, but I think I seriously deserve a medal for my recent actions."

"Herman?" she stretched out his name. "How bad could it be?" Before he could answer, she added, "What did you learn?"

"Besides an elderly man with money is still a hot commodity in the senior single scene?"

"I was looking for something else. With women outliving men, of course a man like yourself would be a hot commodity. Did you find out anything about Mabel?"

They rode in silence for a couple of blocks as he gathered what he knew. "Amelia…"

"Amelia, is it? So, you exchanged names?" Amusement colored her tone of voice.

His lips twisted as he considered the name thing. "No, I don't think I gave her my name. When I told her, I could pay cash for a house on her street, she gave me her name."

"Of course she did. Go on."

"Turns out Amelia has a hard time sleeping and was peeking out her windows late last night and saw Mabel packing her car with suitcases and whatnots as if in a hurry. She thought it was an odd time to leave on vacation or even move for that matter. Apparently, not a word was exchanged between the two women."

"Excellent. That's more information than Lance and I could get from peering into the house. Sounds like Mabel was in a hurry and anxious to get out of town. I'd say she and Makowski are not good friends. It means *she* probably didn't tell him, but someone did."

The thought that he was the one who unearthed vital information caused him to puff out his chest some. Without him, this would have been a wasted trip. "Did you get anything?"

"Uh huh—a copy of the life insurance policy on Sue Ellen and proof the claim was paid out."

That meant this trip wasn't all him. Still, Marcy had connections he didn't have. "How much?"

"Two million. I know it sounds like a lot but not much for the wealthy set. It was taken out just over two years before the suicide. There was the usual two years suicide clause. Makes you wonder."

Herman knew what she was hinting at—the husband somehow being involved. It was obvious. Still, the one thing he'd learned helping Mark and Donna solve crimes in Legacy was the most obvious suspect was never the culprit. "You think Sue Ellen signed that form?"

Marcy glanced out the window, observing the passing scenery before speaking. "It would make me nervous. What was it that Jay Gatsby said—something about the rich being different from us? Maybe this was some type of concession. She knew he wasn't going to be in the will, but he didn't, until the very end when he found out."

The more they dug, the more they found, which made everything even more convoluted than before. "Wouldn't an insurance agent have to see Sue Ellen sign the papers?"

"Normally, yes. If they used the same agent for everything, he could trust Makowski to get the papers signed and brought back to him. If it isn't her signature, there's a possibility the insurance agent was in on it, too."

The thought boggled his mind. Who else would step out of the shadows as a member of the conspiracy to kill off a wealthy socialite who just wanted to help homeless dogs and cats have a place to live. "This is beginning to sound like one of those movies where almost everyone is guilty by association. What about the chief? The one who told your friend to write it off as a suicide?"

"That's all I've been thinking about." Her fisted hand went up to her mouth, then she dropped it. "My first question would be why was the investigation squashed? It's better to be thorough the first time. You can't recheck the scene later. My second question would be what was in it for him?"

No need for Herman to point out that those with great responsibility had an even better opportunity to misuse it.

Chapter Seventeen

THE AROMA OF chocolate cookies permeated the area around the computer. Lola glanced at Jake, who was bathed in the blue light of the screen. While she was no computer expert, she'd never come across a desk unit or laptop that smelled like food. The office was Jake's niece, Katie's. She twisted around to see if there was a plate of cookies somewhere. "Did your niece bring in cookies?"

She kind of hoped she did since the only polite thing would be to share. Lately, the only dessert they had was some dark, flavorless mess labeled *pudding*. It wasn't. A cookie would hit the spot.

"Katie. Ha! No cookies for her. That girl's convinced she's fat. Trying to starve herself to look like one of those stick-thin models. The females of today." He added a sniff, finishing his opinion.

If it wasn't cookies, maybe it was one of those scented candles that smelled like food. It always was a bit of a letdown to come to a house that smelled like cinnamon rolls and have her mouth watering in anticipation of the gooey sweet concoction, only to find out it was a candle. "Do you think she has a scented candle that smells like cookies?"

"Nope." Jake didn't even look up from his scrolling. "It's against the fire code. Found out when they took my candle away."

Well, that didn't answer anything. If she were a sleuth—albeit an amateur one—she should be able to solve the mystery of the cookie smell. Jake mumbled something that had Lola leaning closer to see what would cause such a reaction. There was a grainy black and white newspaper photo of Makowski and a woman who she assumed was Jill Olsen. The cookie smell wafted off Jake, in particular, his face. Aha!

"Been baking cookies lately?"

The man shot her a sly look. "You know good and well there's no kitchenettes in our units. Only those in the H unit have the privilege of a full-size fridge and stove."

She heaved a sigh knowing how close-mouthed Jake could be. If someone was supplying him with goodies, he'd never tell. Even worse, he wasn't sharing. "Have you charmed a lady friend into sending you cookies?"

He laughed, and a roguish twinkle appeared in his eyes. "Lola, as a woman of the world, you know I can't divulge that information as a gentleman."

She gave a derisive snort. It sounded like an excuse for not sharing. Jake's mysteriousness had some of the women gaga about him, but it could be just a smokescreen for selfishness. If a man wouldn't share his cookies, what else was he not splitting among his friends?

Jake tapped the computer screen. "Is this what you're looking for?"

It was an announcement about a new business Makowski was starting, some firm with an environmental name that was supposed to hire disenfranchised veterans. The man's big, toothy grin reminded her of the wolf in "The Little Red Riding Hood." Most of the characters in the tale were taken in by the wolf pretending to be nice when he had ulterior motives. The date on the paper was March 2012, which was after the death of his wife. The woman standing in the background looked a little less like Marian the Librarian. She'd lost her glasses, and her neckline was significantly lower. It also appeared her figure had blossomed, possibly under the hands of a plastic surgeon.

"What does Makowski do for a living? I don't remember it being anything environmental. He doesn't strike me as the type."

"Me, either," Jake agreed and scrolled through the article. "It refers to him as investor and financier. That could mean anything, from loan shark to investment banker. What it comes down to is he plays with other people's money."

"Makes sense. The quickest way to make money is to take other people's money. A bit like the casino with the only difference being now and then, someone wins big."

"There have to be investors who do well with investments to encourage others to invest."

She pursed her lips as she considered the photo. "It should be easy enough to fake superior returns for a few important investors. More than one money manager has done it while shuffling all the rest of the money into his offshore accounts."

That wasn't what she hoped to find in the photos. If the man was doing well financially, he'd have no reason to sell his wife's expensive ring. She'd even attended a funeral where the relatives stripped the woman of the jewelry she was laid out in. Their excuse was the funeral home employees would do likewise before they closed the casket. "Do you remember if the notes said anything about where Sue Ellen is buried?"

The sound of paper turning indicated Jake was searching for the information. "I'm betting they won't allow us to dig the woman up on some suspicion you might have. I know they do it all the time on television. Still, that is television." His finger stopped on a line. "Okay. Here it is. Sue Ellen was cremated. Who knows where her ashes might be? There's no standing memorial that anyone can go to in an effort to pay their respects."

"Figures." She made a derisive snort.

Jake glanced up. "Obviously, you think you know something."

"No *body*."

"That's what cremation is."

"No autopsy."

"The woman was missing half her head. It was obvious what killed her."

"I'd be more interested if there were any drugs in her system. It's a well-known fact that women don't commit suicide by shooting themselves. Too painful. Messy. What if you do it wrong? Then you'll just be hooked up to some machines for the rest of your life and be a drain on your family."

"Do you think she drugged herself?"

"Possibly. I don't know. Without an autopsy, it's hard to say. Someone could have drugged her, making her less likely to fight back."

"Good point. Burning the evidence does make things appear suspicious." He stroked his clean-shaven chin with his hand. "Still, cremation is much more popular than it used to be."

"Maybe. Maybe not. I smell a rat. Take a look at the photo." Lola pointed out the woman in the back. "It's Jill. He's still making her stand in the background. He's smart enough to know she might be a liability as opposed to an asset. I'm willing to bet people never knew he remarried. Probably worked the image of a grieving widower for umpteen years. Gus knows about the marriage from searching public records. I've known plenty of men who never wore wedding rings or mentioned their wives in conversation. I'd like to see some close-up photos."

Jake turned away from the screen and gave her a long look that ended with an eyebrow lift. "You do understand Makowski and new wife aren't exactly celebrities. It's not like the paper would plaster their faces everywhere."

Yes, she knew that, but he was missing the obvious. She gestured to the computer. "Go to the social media site. The one that used to be popular with the teens, but now is not once their parents started using it."

"I think I know the one you mean." He typed in a few letters and an image appeared on the screen. "I'm not sure what you think this will do for you?"

"Ha! Not the Mr.-Know-It-All you think you are." Okay, she'd admit that was petty. It kinda irked her the way Jake held himself aloof as if he were somehow superior to everyone. It felt good to know something he didn't. "Police and insurance investigators are monitoring social media to catch criminals all the time. They can't help bragging about it."

Jake didn't give her a condescending smile or even the superior eyebrow lift. Instead, he asked in a bored tone, "I will repeat my question in a different manner. This helps us how?"

"It's obvious that Makowski wants his new wife out of the lime-light. My bet is Jill worked too hard to get where she is. Half the fun of travel, going to expensive restaurants, paying too much for clothes and spa treatments is bragging about it. It's probably more than half. Anyhow, who can she show off to when her husband won't even acknowledge her publicly? All she has is her friends or cyber friends. I'm willing to bet the woman has a public account because she wants people to *know*. If her husband finds out, she can claim she knows nothing about security."

Jake typed a few words into the search bar. "Do you have any clue how many Jill Olsens there are on this site?"

"Add her married name. She would have," Lola instructed.

For a man who acted like he knew so much, he missed the basic fact that if a woman wanted to brag about her marriage, she'd include her married name and lots of photos to back up her claims. With any luck the photos would be incriminating somehow. She wasn't sure. None of them featured Makowski holding a gun to his wife's head.

A few more key clicks occurred before Jake announced, "I think this is it. Take a look."

There was a photo of a grinning woman with her arms wrapped around a man who was obviously Makowski but was looking away from the camera. The site was loaded with an endless parade of photos of different dishes they'd eaten at various restaurants and shots of Jill sunning at various resorts and on a yacht, too. What was missing were photos of the loving couple together. There was one photo buried in between Jill's shopping sprees and a Himalayan cat named Tootles. A shot of her holding up her right hand with a massive diamond on it.

"There's your ring," Jake pointed out.

It could be helpful since she was certain the ring would tell her what she needed to know. "You're right. It's a doozy. Notice it's on her right hand and not her left."

"Saw that. Would a woman want to wear an engagement ring from a previous wife? Never mind the bad vibes from taking the ring off a suicide."

That gave her pause. Most curses appeared to focus on sizable diamonds such as The Hope Diamond. "I don't know any women who'd accept a cast-off from another woman. It means the man didn't make an effort. It also means he found the two women interchangeable, and no one wants that."

A snort erupted from Jake, followed by a guffaw. "You got me there. Obviously, you know much more about women and rings than I do. It's obvious Jill does have the ring even though she's not sporting it on her left hand. What does that tell you?"

It should tell her something. The most obvious answer was the woman needed to show off to anyone who would look at her online profile. People in the surrounding area might not know Jill was married, but there might be thousands of people envying her around the globe. "How many friends does she have? It's there on her profile near the top."

"Thought you didn't know much about computers," Jake grumbled as he scrolled upward.

"I don't. You can get the social media feeds on your phone. My friend helped me set up an account. Played a few games using the account, but then I forgot about it. I did notice all the fake posts where husbands and wives tell each other online how much they love each other as if they don't live in the same house and go to sleep next to one another every night. Why do you do that unless it's to impress someone else?"

"Good point. Jill has a hundred and one friends."

"It's an open account?"

"As far as I can tell."

"Let's befriend her."

"You need an account."

"I have one. It's under Lola Feathers."

"Feathers?" He wrinkled his nose.

"Stage name. Just type it in. We'll open my account. Look up Jill and put out a friend request."

Jake's right hand went up to rub the back of his neck. "I don't know about this, Lola. I'm not sure Marcy would approve."

"There's no way it can be traced back to me, or Marcy, for that matter."

Lola's page came up with a banner of showgirl legs and an inset photo of when she was twenty years old. The profile went on to list her occupation as showgirl and locale as Vegas. Jake read over it and looked at her. "You're right! No one will connect it to you."

Chapter Eighteen

G US WAS THE last one to dash into the office. He accompanied his entrance with a vocal *swoosh* as if sliding into home plate. Marcy closed the door and pivoted her chair to face Jake, who was still on the computer. "It was nice of your niece to allow us to use her office."

He twisted a little in his chair to face Marcy. "Yeah, she's a good kid. She told me she needed a break, which is code for walking to H Unit and talking to the new male nurse they recently hired."

He batted his eyes and pursed his lips, causing Lola to react. "Cut that out! You're not being funny. Katie is a grown woman within kissing distance of forty. Give her as much respect as she gives you."

"You're right." He hung his head.

Marcy shook her head, then cleared her throat. "All right, this meeting is called to order. Does anyone have anything to report?"

Gus, who had perched on the edge of the desk, jumped up. "I do! Eunice and I had a wonderful interview with the newspaper guy. Gotta give the old girl credit because she saved some of the slop they've been passing off as food. Newspaper guy couldn't believe it was recent food. He'd never seen mashed potatoes that color before. Told him, neither had I."

"I'm glad your interview went well, but I meant about our case," Marcy commented.

Gus took that as his cue to keep talking. "Interview wasn't that long. I showed him the bad food, told him how long it had been going on and had our photo taken. Left me plenty of time to do some scouting on Jill Olsen Makowski. I found nothing except she's forty-seven and was born in Park County. She went to school, graduated, and attended college for two years. Worked data entry at a local company before snagging the job with Makowski. Never married before snagging him. The one thing I noticed was her lack of volunteerism and being associated with any local organization."

It looked like he was through, but before Marcy could call on anyone else, he held one finger up. "I looked her up on social media."

Lola interrupted, "We looked her up on social media!" She put one balled hand on her hip, clutched her walker with the other, and glared at Gus. "Jake and I discovered the missing blue diamond in one of her photos. Not much else except endless photos of her sunning in various exotic locales. That woman's skin is probably as tough as a saddle by now. What was most noticeable about the shots was the lack of her husband."

Gus's forehead puckered as if trying to figure out something. "That's not the one I was on. I looked her up by her full name—Jill Rosalie Olsen."

"Rosalie..." Lola repeated the middle name, then looked at Jake who was typing. He turned back to her.

"Got it. This must have been put up when she was much younger. Under groups, she's listed as a member of the Backstreet Boys Forever Fan Club."

"Go on..." Gus urged.

"Fashions R Us."

Lola clicked her tongue. "That can't be right. I'd never accuse the woman of being fashionable."

"I think I found it. The Golddiggers 101 Club?"

"That's it! Obviously, the woman was training to be the wife of a wealthy man. All she needed was a wealthy bachelor."

Marcy tapped the arm of her chair as she reviewed the mental information. "Here's what we have. A woman who wanted to marry well, which is probably about half of the female population. She does marry well. Then, she flashes a well-known diamond on the Internet. None of these are actually punishable offenses."

Her announcement had the same effect as stomping on a flower. Gus and Lola sighed and collapsed back into their seats—a little on the wilted side. "Still..." Lola began. She turned slightly to address Jake. "Pull up that site we were looking at earlier."

She pivoted to the group. "We've all heard that the will left nothing to the husband. The big diamond would not have been his to give to his newest squeeze."

Marcy frowned. "True. It would take the Humane Society suing for the ring, which takes money they don't have. You'd also have to produce the ring, too. I can well imagine that it would be..." Marcy held up her fingers to make air quotes, "...lost." She closed the quotes.

Lola shook her head emphatically. "Not my point. I went back and looked at the photo of Sue Ellen. I had to use my magnifying glass, but you could see the white strip of skin where her ring should have been. A sign of a woman who never took off her ring, which brings me back to who decided to swipe the ring off a dead woman?"

"Husband could have..." Herman volunteered. "At the time, no one knew about the will yet."

"True, but according to the notes..." Marcy began, "he arrived after the police. Once there the police secured the scene and would not let a grieving husband divest his wife of valuable jewels. It doesn't sound like something a shocked spouse would do. He comes in, throws up his hands, then goes for the jewelry. Not hardly."

"That only leaves Mabel or the murderer…" Jake surmised, looking a trifle smug at his deduction.

"Maybe…" Lola conceded. "We still don't know if Makowski did it or how Jill is involved in all of this."

Herman rubbed at the furrows in his forehead with two fingers as he spoke. "Not sure why you two are focusing on Jill. It's not unusual for a successful man to marry a younger woman."

Even though Marcy knew something wasn't right about the case, she hadn't sorted it out yet. It was hard to shake that mental fog that slipped in at the most inconvenient times. "Got a theory, Jake? Lola?"

"Yes!" They answered in unison, but Jake slipped out of his chair and gestured to the monitor. "Jill is not a bad looking woman. She may be in her forties but doesn't look it."

"Thanks to expensive plastic surgeons. She looks better now than she did ten years ago…" Lola interjected.

A whistle cut the air as Gus moved close. "I know there's some new equipment there that wasn't installed in the photos I was looking at earlier."

Jake held up his hand to continue. "What husband would ignore his younger, attractive wife? Most men would make sure to be in every photo with his arm possessively around her waist. In the profile shot, the husband is looking away. Jill may have crept up to him and took a selfie without him even being aware. This is a man who doesn't want to be with his younger wife, which is odd."

Lola made a low sound of dissent, causing Jake to twirl and ask, "What?"

"He had no trouble spending money on her."

"That might be to keep her quiet. It puzzles me that Makowski chose to marry his assistant, then told no one about it. He tries not to be photographed with Jill. No one would think it peculiar that a widower would re-marry. Not even too surprising that he married someone he knew already. Most men would take the opportunity to showcase a younger wife."

The pieces were starting to come together. Even though she had solicited the help of her fellow residents, it was important that she came up with the information. "It means Makowski is being blackmailed by Jill. As the assistant, it would have been easy enough for her to stumble across something that may have made her suspicious." Lola raised her eyebrows. "It could have been the insurance paperwork."

"That was filed more than two years ago…" Lola pointed out. Before anyone could comment, she continued, "It could be that Jill decided to play the long game. Somehow, she got a peek at the papers and decided to wait for the opportunity to act on it."

It was a possibility. It would help if she could examine the signature on the insurance paper. "Lance gave me a copy of the insurance form."

Herman harrumphed, attracting attention. "Where would we get a copy of Sue Ellen's signature?"

"We're in luck." Marcy's mood lifted knowing she was close to solving the case. "My mother was a volunteer for the rescue society. Sue Ellen made a point to send every volunteer a birthday card. My mother kept every one of them." She blew out a breath knowing what was ahead. "I'll have to head to the storage facility where mother's stuff is stored. It'll be a big job, but I'll have to do it."

Herman moved closer to Marcy, then squatted to be eye to eye with the woman. "What you mean is *we* will do it. Work divided is work lessened."

Chapter Nineteen

HERMAN WAITED NEAR the front doors for Marcy and the rest of the crew. A quick glance at the wall clock showed that the fellow members of the team were late. Sure, he might expect Jake or even Gus to be late, but never Marcy, who saw punctuality as a good trait. Still, something was up.

The clarion siren sounded. The fire alarm lights flashed as two staffers wandered into the hallway, peering around.

"Do you think this is a real one?"

"There was no mention of having a drill. They hardly ever do that because it takes too long to get everyone out of the place."

"True. Do you think we should do anything?"

"I don't know. We should report to our station just in case we have to escort the residents outside."

The employees vanished from view at a fast walk. Herman edged toward the door, not certain if he should be outside just in case there might be a fire for real. Outside, there was a whine of firetrucks and a grumble of their engines. Where was everyone?

As if his thoughts conjured him, Gus came tearing around the corner waving his hands. "It's a fire. Everyone out!"

A few startled residents joined him and surged toward the front doors. Herman jumped out of the way. Lola came around the corner with Marcy beside her.

"Let me do it! I can do it myself better than you can."

Jake, who had been attempting to push Marcy's chair, held up his hands and followed. The three of them exited out the front door followed by dozens of residents, a few still clutching bingo cards.

It was hard to say what was going on, but Herman recognized an opportunity when he saw one and followed the group. The bingo players gathered on the lawn and grumbled about how the game should be restarted. Firemen charged down the sidewalk, causing one woman to clap.

"That's more like it! No one told me hot firemen would be our treat today."

Herman rushed to his car, not waiting around to hear more. It explained why he hadn't struck up any acquaintances of the female gender. Apparently, they were holding out for hot firemen. By the time he reached his car where the crew was waiting, he wasn't in the best of moods. He opened the car and trunk to facilitate everyone getting in. Thankfully, there was no fire engine blocking his way.

The back of his seat vibrated under Marcy's hand slaps. "Go! Go! Now! Before they find out the fire alarm was fake."

Fake. He wanted to ask what the deal was, but he needed to concentrate on weaving his way through the parking lot without attracting too much attention, which might be somewhat harder than usual due to the multitude of folks standing outside.

He made it to the main thoroughfare before asking the obvious. "What's up with the fake fire alarm?"

Lola sighed, then spat one word, "Eunice."

Of course, he should have known. Whenever trouble appeared, Eunice was near. "She pulled the alarm?"

"No. She pointed out to the activity director that we hadn't done anything as far as organizing the dance. The woman snagged us as we tried to leave. We were stuck having to talk about music and decorations knowing you were waiting."

"How did you get away?"

There was some discussion in the back seat, not loud enough for Herman to hear, but he had the feeling no one knew what happened. To be clear, he asked again, raising his voice to be heard above the chatter. "Did Eunice pull the fire alarm or what?"

The backseat discussion quieted in time for Gus to be heard. "I pulled it. What a grand plan. Told the activity director I had to go to the restroom. After I pulled it, I ran through the halls yelling 'Fire! Fire!' to confuse the matter some. You may have noticed how many residents actually made their way outside."

There *had* been some folks already on the grass as they exited the scene. He cut his eyes to his army buddy who was grinning like a Cheshire Cat. "You do know people will suspect you?"

"Au contraire." He tapped his index finger against his forehead. 'That's why I was running through the halls, yelling. No one would do that if he had pulled the alarm."

Jake commented from the back seat. "A crazy person would."

Gus continued to grin, which meant he must not have heard the man. Still, Herman worried about the fallout after such an incident. "What about the residents? Don't you think the excitement of a possible fire might be too much for them?"

Instead of his friend answering, Lola raised her voice loud enough for Gus to hear. "The excitement would do them some good. It was probably the first time some of them had been outside in months, maybe years. At least the breeze will blow the funk off them."

"Outside?" Gus replied and pivoted to address those seated behind him. "We're outside now."

Herman sucked in his lips. The Gus he remembered had always

been a jokester, a lover of practical jokes. Too often, the man *did* hear what he shouldn't have heard if he were truly hard of hearing. How did he pick out the word *outside* in a sentence? Most people caught the first word because people tended to emphasize it as they started a sentence. Voices often grew softer as the sentence went on, making the last word difficult to decipher.

Any time now, the man would flash his goofy grin and inform them he could hear all the time. Then he'd laugh at them. Not Herman though. He'd be able to mention this time and how he knew Gus could hear. The joke would be on him since he chose to say nothing. Hard to believe he was the one who married out of the three of them. Gus's wife, Mary, must have been able to tolerate a joke. Oddly, Gus almost never mentioned her.

When Herman first arrived at the home, he met many residents who talked about their spouses as if they were in the next room. Jake had to inform him that most of the mentioned spouses were no longer on this side of the soil. Even those poor souls who were hanging onto memories of their departed spouse, he envied. They had memories of a love, a life shared, whereas, he didn't.

A thump on the seat rattled him, causing him to ease off the gas. "What?"

"Where are you going?" Jake had leaned forward in the asking to breathe his cookie breath on Herman.

He tried to brush it away with his hand. "Get back. I don't you need you breathing down my neck. You keep wolfing down those sweets, and you'll no longer have a svelte figure. As for where I'm going, we're headed to Marcy's storage unit."

"Herman!" Marcy called out. "I didn't tell you where it was."

"Oh." That meant he was driving mindlessly, lost in his thoughts. How embarrassing. The last thing he wanted was to be labeled as having a senior moment. People of all ages forgot stuff. His grandniece, Gwen, was always misplacing items. However, when she did it, it was because she was preoccupied as if she had all the weighty matters of the world on her shoulders. Usually, it was a boy who put that uncomprehending look on her face, not world peace. When he missed a snippet of conversation, people viewed him rather like a blank cassette tape, out of date and having no content. An empty church parking lot beckoned as a stopping point. It would have been better for him to be clear on the directions before proceeding.

Herman put on his blinker and turned into the parking lot, which caused Gus to chirp, "Are we stopping here so you can pray for a clue?"

The man chuckled at his own inane remark. It was tempting to open the door and kick him out. Herman considered the possibility for two heartbeats but realized he didn't have enough friends that he could afford to lose any, no matter how irritating they could be at times. The three of them became men with bullets zooming overhead and the mission to save their country and others from world dominance by a crazed dictator. There was never any room for tenderness or even compassion. Soldiers kept their heads down and fired back. At least, the others did. His kinder, gentler nature must have come from the fact he spent his wartime in Panama, enjoying the tropical climate while keeping the canal open for the Allied Forces.

He never let on how pleasurable his tour of duty was. How could he when Gus spent most of his time almost getting blown to Kingdom Come and Jake ran covert missions behind enemy lines that would have ended in torture if caught. Nope, no one would want to hear how he improved his poker bluffing and enjoyed the local Seco liquor that was served with milk over ice.

The sedan bumped into what he thought was an empty parking lot only to have a woman shoot out of the building and jog toward their car.

The stout woman waved, which forced Herman to roll down the window. It was the only polite thing to do considering he was in her parking lot. He cleared his throat. "Sorry. We were lost and pulled in here to get clear on the directions."

"No problem. The church is a great place for those who are lost. It's the perfect place for lost souls." The woman chuckled, causing the reading glasses on her nose to bounce. "Reverend Lenora Banks." She held out her hand.

Herman shifted the car into park to shake her hand. He expected a woman minister would have a delicate grasp. The woman squeezed his hand for all it was worth, then gave it a vigorous pump. What had she done in a previous life? Wrestle alligators?

Marcy interrupted the greeting session. "Hello, Reverend Banks. We actually know where we're going. Herman took a wrong turn."

The minister released Herman's hand. He withdrew it into the car, dropped it below window level and gave it a little shake.

Lenora nodded. "Many have taken the wrong turn on life's highway."

Not knowing how to answer, he didn't. Gus did. "We're on the county road, not a highway. We don't need to be on a highway. We aren't going that far."

As Gus continued to ramble about roads versus highways, Marcy called out instructions. "Let's go. Take a left out of the parking lot. Everyone wave at the minister."

Herman put up his hand to wave but decided against it. Probably best not to wave being the driver.

It didn't take them long to get to the storage unit, which was good. Once the garage style door went up, they saw the multitude of boxes and knew how the rest of the day would be spent.

Lola moved forward and gestured to the boxes. "For pity's sake, was there nothing of your mother's that you threw away?"

Not answering right away, Marcy wheeled her way into the unit and pointed to the far wall. "There're four folding chairs over there you can pull out and use. Mother's bridge set." She glanced back at Lola, "This isn't everything by a long shot. Most of the furniture went to the DAV. I packed up the clothes and dropped them off at the local thrift shop. Some of the stuff, such as her jewelry and a few books, I took home." She gestured to the stacked boxes. "This stuff I never had time to go through since her house sold the day I put it on the market. I ended up moving the boxes to this storage unit for when I had time to go through everything and see what was valuable and what to discard. Then I had the accident. The rest you know."

It was hard to know how to reply to that. Herman only nodded.

After Jake unearthed chairs for them to sit on, Marcy decided they'd make a pile for the dumpster, another to drop off at Goodwill, but under no circumstance was any card or letter to end up in either pile.

Two hours later, Gus held up an object that bore some resemblance to a caulking gun. "What's this?"

Marcy glanced up from paging through a photo album. "Cookie shooter. My mother was very much into cookies when she wasn't helping to raise money for homeless pups."

"Keep?" Gus wiggled the item in the air. "I happen to know your mother isn't the only one interested in cookies." He directed a look in Jake's direction.

"Giveaway pile. Not too many people bother to make homemade cookies, but there's a few."

After working through a collection of vinyl records by artists long since dead and a huge collection of dog figurines, Herman opened a box, which appeared to be nightgowns. He almost put it aside for one of the women to inspect when he felt something shift in the bottom. He lifted out a pretty floral gown to reveal bundles of rubber-banded cards.

"I think I found it."

Chapter Twenty

THE SMELL THAT wafted out the front doors made Marcy wonder if there had been an actual fire. Despite Gus confessing to pulling the fire alarm, something smelled off. Gus bumped into her when she halted in the middle of the door.

"Hold on." She sniffed the air again and wondered if it would be too late to go back to the storage unit, which only smelled slightly musty. "I'm trying to decide what the horrible smell is."

"Lunch." He snorted. "They burned it, too. We should have picked up something while we were out."

"I agree."

The sound of voices behind them meant someone else was coming up the walk. Jake and Lola were strolling up the path. Might as well move out of the way. She maneuvered the chair to the side while she assured herself the farther she got from the dining room the less the odor would be. Surely, they'd never serve something they'd burned. Next time out, she'd make a point of stopping by a store to pick up some snacks she could store in her room.

"What should we do now?" Jake directed the question to Gus, who shrugged and pointed to the dining room.

They waited until Herman arrived and headed to Marcy's room, which happened to be the one farthest from the dining room. Once they arrived, she'd get Herman to open a few windows. Thank goodness the place was an older home that had windows that actually opened. Not too far though, since residents might leave via the window. Of course, the home insisted it was because they didn't want anyone to enter from the outside.

Inside Marcy's room, she extracted the copy of the application for the insurance policy and compared it to one of the birthday cards Sue Ellen sent. They looked pretty similar. *Drat.* Not what she wanted to see. "Turn on the overhead light, please."

Herman did her bidding, but it didn't improve the identification. Lola moved closer. "Most people write differently depending on how they feel. If tired or there is too little space, the signature might be sloppy or cramped."

"Isn't there some type of expert you can consult?" Herman gestured to the letter.

"There is. Costs money, though. We aren't actually allowed to spend money on the case. This was supposed to be solved on information that was already collected."

"What information?" Lola placed a fist on her hip as she balanced against the wall. "Outside of a few photos, we looked up everything."

"True. Even if we did have money, those handwriting analysis experts take time. We don't have time since Makowski is emigrating."

Jake shot a hand through his hair and grimaced. "Can't Lance do something?"

She sucked in her lips. The whole reason she even had the case was no one had time or inclination to pursue what had been ruled a suicide. "Not sure. Chief Emmett Watson ruled it a suicide. Closed it."

"Wait." Herman held up a finger. "Isn't he the retired chief?"

"He is, but that doesn't mean he spends his days fishing. He keeps his ears open. I figure whatever made him decide to do Makowski a favor and not investigate the case still holds."

"What a load of bull!" Lola shook her head. "I thought when I moved here I got away from all the corrupt officials."

"You're never away from corruption. As long as there is greed, there's corruption. I like to think it's a case of a friend doing a favor for another friend as opposed to a crime coverup, which would be a felony."

"Yeah, I can see why you might want to think that," Jake added, while Gus worked his way closer to the table where the paper and card laid.

He picked up the card and flourished it. "Get out the other cards. I want to examine them. I'm pretty good at handwriting analysis. I'll need a paper and a pen, too."

Once the items were assembled, Gus studied the application, then the cards. He picked up the pen and made several cursive E's, S's, and M's, then he wrote *Sue Ellen Makowski* several times until he came up with one he liked. He folded the paper to hide the rest of his attempts, then pushed it next to the policy. "Compare."

The four of them hunched over the paper, causing a shadow at the same time. "I can't see anything," Marcy complained. It took a few minutes for everyone to peer at the paper. Amazingly, it looked just the same. "Gus, how did you manage to mimic Sue Ellen's signature? Were you a forger?"

"Forger, hah! Harsh appellation for a fun activity. By the way, I was only emulating a forged signature, which is easier than an actual one."

"What?" It looked the same to her. "How do you know it's forged?"

Gus cleared his throat, then pointed at the policy signature. "Do you see that each letter shows the same amount of pressure?"

She hadn't. On second look, they *were* uniform. On the other hand, the signatures on the cards became lighter as they went on, and on some cards the *i* at the end of Makowski was little more than a tiny line with no upward swoop or even a dot above it. "I do now."

"That's because…" he grinned and held up his hand, "…wait for it."

Jake jostled the man. "Get on with it."

"We all know our names. We don't think about it when signing. Sometimes, when people are in a hurry, they even misspell their own names. No one would carefully stare at the paper, making sure to keep the pressure and letter size uniform unless he or she was trying to forge someone's signature."

Lola reached for a birthday card and held it up to the policy application. "Once you pointed it out, it's obvious. Someone who knew her signature well could have tried a little harder. Makes me wonder if this was a rushed job or an impulse decision." She tapped her finger on the third name on the list. "Look, the insurance agent is Charles Makowski, who I'm willing to bet is a relative."

"The plot thickens," Herman mused and stroked his chin the way he'd seen Detective Taber do while pondering a case development. "I imagine our suspect is the more influential member of the family. If he said he'd return the paper signed, nothing more would be said about it."

"Then Sue Ellen dies. Charles might not think much about it since it's been a few years." Jake pivoted slowly to meet everyone's eyes. He had to crouch to catch Gus's attention. "If he's suspicious, he can't do anything because it looks like he's complicit."

Gus nodded, signaling he heard, while Marcy asked the obvious, "I can see that. The big question is, what to do now?"

Everyone stared back at her. As the professional, she should have an answer, but she didn't. In some ways, she was surprised she'd gotten this far. "It wasn't a rhetorical question. I was asking you guys what to do."

No answer. An unexpected, but familiar voice called out. "Do about what?"

Eunice. Just what they didn't need—a visit from their resident busybody. Gus must have sensed everyone's attention shift since he turned slowly and spotted the intruder. "Eunice." He popped up from his seat beside the cards. "We need to talk. Have you been past the dining room?"

The woman gave a slow nod, possibly surprised by this new version of Gus who appeared to be all business. He maneuvered around the others to reach his target and locked arms with Eunice. "Let's go plan how we will handle this latest outrage. I think we should demand pizza delivery."

"Ooh, pizza! That sounds good."

Marcy watched the two of them exit the room. "Do you think we'll get pizza?"

"Depends if forgery is involved," Jake joked, making the rest of them laugh.

She held up her hand for attention. "I hate to proceed without Gus, but we don't have time to twiddle our thumbs. Mabel has left town, obviously afraid of something."

"Getting caught." Lola shook her finger. "It would have been easy for her to slip that ring off a dead woman's finger."

"Since she found the woman, she'd have the most access. If she did, why didn't Makowski report the ring missing?"

Herman held up his hand.

"We're not in school." Marcy grinned at the silver maned man.

"What is it?"

"Well…" he started, then shifted his pose to cross his arms and lean against the door. Unfortunately, Gus hadn't totally closed the door, and it shifted underneath Herman, causing the man to scramble to grab the doorsill before he met the floor. He stood gripping the frame before pulling himself upright. Lola was the first to respond.

"Are you okay?"

"Only my pride was hurt." He moved to lean against the wall. "Domestics know quite a bit about the families they work for. It could be Mabel knew something. Whatever it was had Makowski facilitating her early retirement."

"Could be." Jake joined both of his hands together and clasped them. "Mabel and Makowski could have been an item."

Marcy shook her head. The woman didn't strike her as a femme fatale. "If that were the case, why did he marry Jill?"

"Some men are like that. They won't settle for just one woman."

"I've known my share," Lola added. "I wonder if the little wifey, Jill, is emigrating to Ireland. I think it's time to see if she accepted my friend request."

"Even if she did, you can't just ask her that." Herman's eyebrows lifted at the suggestion.

"I would never ask her. She'll tell me because she can't resist bragging, especially to a former showgirl. She's got to prove her more adventurous life."

A twinkle appeared in the woman's eyes, making Marcy consider that they just might unveil Sue Ellen's murderer—hopefully in time.

Chapter Twenty-One

KATIE GRINNED AT the group when they showed up at her office. She held up her index finger and wagged it in their direction as she spoke. "I don't mind helping you, but this can't be an everyday thing. Maybe you can pool your funds and buy a laptop." Her eyes rolled upward, and her mouth opened the tiniest little bit.

Both of Katie's hands slapped her desk. "I know what I can do! I have a laptop I'm not using. It's not the latest model, but if ya'all aren't using it to play online games, it should work. What do you think, Uncle Jake?"

"Oh, I don't think…"

Lola elbowed him before he could refuse and hissed, "Take it."

After solving this case, which they had almost figured out, with the exception of fingering the murderer, there would be others. This was the most fun she'd had at the home since the 4-H group came back to talk about their projects and the baby piglets got loose. It took forever for them to round up the runaways. Almost everyone got a visit from a porcine escape artist.

Jake gave her a reproachful look for the elbow, then announced, "Sure, sounds good."

"All right. I'll write myself a note to bring it." She clasped her hands and stretched them over her head. "My goodness, all this sitting makes me sleepy. I need a walk to wake myself up."

The rest of the group shared smiles, well aware of where Katie was going. As she reached the door, Jake added, "Clinton is an outstanding fellow. I checked him out."

"Uncle Jake!" Her eyebrows shot up, then she laid a hand over her heart as her brows returned to their natural position. "Thanks. You saved me some money."

Lola gave Jake a speculative look after his niece left.

"What?" He moved toward the computer, his shadow reaching it before he did. "Family has to look after family. Half the time, a female thinks a man is a certain way because he looks good and can lie better than a politician."

"It's nice you're using your skills to help out family. I don't have much family to speak of. Left home early and never looked back. I'm not even sure if I have any nieces or nephews." A long sigh escaped Lola, which she hated since it made her sound pathetic.

No one in her family had begged her to stay. They didn't even bother to look her up after she left. She told herself it was better that way. Her friends were her family. That turned out much better for her. It *had* worked, until her friends started vanishing. Some died, others married, and a few moved to live near their children. It was one of the reasons the idea of moving to a retirement center appealed to her. Here she expected to reinvent herself. Maybe even make up a tragic story about the love of her life dying. That chance never materialized after her friend had been quick to inform everyone about Lola's glittery past. If the ploy was supposed to make her popular, it didn't. Many of the women treated her as if she had leprosy while the men with all their wits were disappointed she wasn't twenty and walking around wearing a feather headdress. Okay, maybe those few didn't have *all* their senses.

The nameless crime solving group brought a sense of purpose to her life. It would be good to put a name to the killer. The boys—and

Marcy—thought it was the husband, but she had worked with women long enough to know they could be as deadly as their male counterparts or deadlier. "Got the computer up yet?"

"No." Jake snorted. "As slow as it is connecting, every other resident must be watching cute cat videos or stalking their grandchildren on social media."

As far as technology went, she felt as if time had left her behind. "At craft time, which was painting flowers on plates, Tilly commented that she'd downloaded her granddaughter's wedding photo and changed out the groom."

A few more keystrokes sounded from the computer area. Herman nosed around the office, picking up magazines and straightening photos. Marcy rolled toward her and asked, "What did she do with the real groom?"

"Don't know." Lola shrugged. "I guess she didn't like the guy her granddaughter married. The way she saw it, if she was going to look at a photo every day it might as well be someone she liked."

"Makes sense. Not sure the granddaughter would see it that way."

"Yeah. People are funny that way. They expect everyone to adore whomever they choose to marry. Most of the time, I could care less who my friends married. After all, I don't have to spend time with them. It only irked me when the man got between me and spending time with my friends. Occasionally, my friends changed due to getting hitched."

"Been there. Done that. What bothered me is when some of my fellow officers married, they quit the force. Made me wonder if that was their plan all along. Find a man, quit the job, or if it was the other way, and the man insisted his wife give up her position."

The sharp sound of Jake clapping his hands together attracted attention. "We have contact! Need your help, Lola, to get into your account."

"Coming." She used the nearby chairs and desks for walking supports as opposed to using her walker in the tight space. If she did fall, she'd either end up on top of someone or sprawled across a desk. After a half a dozen cautious steps, she collapsed into a padded chair next to Jake. "Give me the keyboard."

After typing in her password, her profile came up. Herman hovered near her shoulder and whistled. "Who's the dame?"

Really, this again? "It's me. I was much younger."

"I'll say."

If she had a cane, she could have carelessly let it slip, giving the man a good whack in the shins. It was another argument for a cane. Maybe, if she knew back in the day that if she capitalized on her looks and would be continually judged by them or the lack of them when she was older, she might have opted for veterinarian assistant or any other job that didn't require looking good in heels.

Up in the corner, a glowing number notified her of two messages. *Excellent!* Her plan worked. She tried to click on the box but didn't quite center it. Jake reached for the mouse.

"Let me do it."

Why was it no one thought she could do the simplest things? Her hand clutched the mouse, refusing to release it. "No. Cool your jets. I can do it myself. It's *my* account."

"Makes no matter to me." The brooding lines of his face denied his words.

So be it. Let the man sulk. It would do him good to develop some patience. Her hand still on the mouse, she carefully moved it over the mailbox. No need to have someone else jump in and demand to show her how to do something she could do on her own.

Click. Two messages shimmered into existence. Lola clicked on the first one that had a subject line.

Delighted to See You Online.

She clicked on the letter. It grew big, filling a portion of the screen.

Dear Lola,

We are delighted to see you back on Friend Zone. We've missed you.
   Find lots of new friends with Friend Zone. Enjoy!
   Your Friends at Friend Zone.

"Figures." Herman groaned behind her. "They got junk mail online, too."

"Hear ya," Jake responded. "Look at how many times they used *friend* in the sentence."

"Must be four, maybe five."

Disappointed with the first message, Lola hovered over the second one and clicked while attempting to ignore the boys who were fussing about the word. A little darker font stood out when she clicked on the letter.

Jill Olsen Makowski accepted your friend request.

Underneath the official response, it looked like Jill had typed her own note.

Hi Lola,

Glad to meet you. I'm excited about being your friend.
   Being a Las Vegas showgirl must be very glamorous.
   Looking forward to your posts and pictures.

Jill

"That's going to be awkward…" Herman offered up.

"What's going to be awkward?" Lola huffed a little, not certain why when she managed to do something it didn't receive proper credit. "I made a connection, which was my intention, and more than you guys did. I got an information pipeline to our possible suspect."

He nodded. "I'll give you that. What about photos? Considering yours are a few years out of date."

"It's not like I'm going to post that many. I can just grab some ad photos from the hotels. If I put on a showgirl shot, I'll say it is a friend. It's not like I'm going to be online that long. We just need to know if she's emigrating, too."

She started typing.

Hi Jill,

It's wonderful to hear from you.

Herman leaned over her shoulder. "How will 'wonderful to hear from you' have her confessing she's emigrating?"

Lola put up her hand. "Just stop and let me type. I know what I'm doing."

Her eyes rolled upward as she tried to tap into her former life where she often got gentlemen to buy her overpriced drinks that were actually ginger ale.

My life is dull compared to yours. You've been to so many exotic locales. I envy you. What's your next trip? Tell me and make me drool. Color me green.

Lola.

Herman pointed to the last line. "Why would she want to color you green?"

"It's an expression, as you well know."

"Not one that I ever used." Herman nudged Jake and asked, "Did you ever say color me green?"

"No." He rubbed the bridge of his nose as he mused. "Can't remember asking anyone to color me anything. Did paint the town red on occasion, though."

"Lola, ignore the men…" Marcy instructed and smiled in her direction. "It's a fine letter. Go ahead and send it."

She reread it just to be sure she hadn't made any obvious typos, then hit send. "I wonder how long it will take her to respond?"

Marcy's shoulders went up with a shrug. "Hard to say. Depends on how much she's doing. I doubt she's at home twiddling her thumbs. The bad news is this is about the only option we have left."

There was a commotion near the door as both Eunice and Gus pushed into the room. Marcy made a quick scrabble for any errant file papers.

Eunice moved toward the computer as if pulled by a magnet. "Hey! What are you doing?"

The computer pinged, drawing Lola's attention. It was Jill and apparently, she didn't have much to do because she'd just responded. As much as she wanted to see what she had to say, she minimized the screen.

"Just checking my email."

Eunice squinted. "Looks like you were checking Friend Zone." She pointed back to herself with one hand. "I'm on Friend Zone. I'll send you an invite."

That might complicate things, considering she was conversing with Jill. Marcy chuckled, drawing their notice. "That would be silly to communicate on online when you two could just talk to each other. I'm surprised at you. Haven't you've read about the mental benefits of talking face to face?"

Even though Lola knew that Marcy was trying to turn aside Eunice's invite, it still sounded a lot like scolding and grated just a tiny bit. It was up to her to say something, but when she opened her mouth, someone shouted in the hallway.

"The pizza's here!"

Gus pivoted and headed for the door. He called back over his shoulder. "You better get a move on it. These people haven't had anything decent in weeks. All the pizza will be inhaled."

Eunice lost interest in the conversation and joined the others heading to the dining room. Pizza would be good, but right now, she needed to see what Jill had to say.

Chapter Twenty-Two

T HE APPETIZING SMELL of melted cheese and hot tomato sauce drifted into the room as Herman returned with a pizza box. Marcy looked up from the computer screen and uttered a heartfelt groan and shot the man a grateful look. "Appreciate it. We got a reply from Jill. It's unexpected, to say the least. I wanted to print it out for proof if we needed it. Not that it included anything that would lock anyone up. Unfortunately, the printer isn't in the room. Lola is out in search of the printer since she thinks she knows where my copy went to."

"She probably does. Let me see what the mysterious Jill wrote." He moved closer to read the message aloud.

"'Hello, Lola. I do travel a bit. Usually to warm places with infinity pools and good-looking cabana boys. My latest trip may be longer and chillier than I'd like. We're planning to go visit the Emerald Isle. I hear that sometimes it is so green there that it hurts your eyes. Some of the castles are available to rent. I wouldn't mind being able to say I slept in a castle. LOL.'"

"It's read L.O.L. It means laughing out loud."

Herman hoisted one eyebrow and continued reading. "'With winter not that far away, I prefer someplace hot and that makes those foot-long frozen drinks. I hear the Irish are friendly. Have you ever been to Ireland? Love to hear more about Vegas. What time do you get up if you work all night? T. T. Y. L.' What is that supposed

161

to mean?"

"Talk to you later."

"Why didn't she just write that?"

"It's an accepted abbreviation."

He snorted. "That's what the young folks like yourself say."

Being called a young folk made her chuckle. Yeah, she wished. Back in the day when she was actually young, she couldn't wait to be older. Looks like she got her wish. "Thanks for linking me to the millennials or whomever you meant."

"You're part of the younger generation in my eyes."

Before she could find some way to denounce his claim, Lola entered the room, pushing her walker with renewed energy. "I got it. Finally. It took some finagling on my part."

Marcy allowed the woman to work her way to a chair before asking for the paper. "The paper?"

"Here it is." She pulled it from the pouch attached to her walker. "One of the aides was printing out coupons. I had to tell her I was looking for a love letter from an admirer. She let me look through her coupons. It was wedged between toilet tissue and soda."

Herman plucked the paper from Lola's hand and stared at it.

"It's the same thing you just read to me," Marcy told him.

He didn't look up from the paper, but mumbled, which she wasn't sure was for her or to himself. "Thought I'd take another look at this. Couldn't see how it would be useful."

Civilians believed solving a crime was something that can be done in sixty minutes or less depending on the number of commercials. It was more like a five-thousand-piece jigsaw puzzle that had more than a handful of pieces missing. There was a reason many crimes remained unsolved or took years to solve. Over in California, a serial killer was arrested after being on the lam for forty years.

"It doesn't mention that Jill heard her husband admit to killing his former wife. It just gave us a little more information that we didn't have."

Lola gave Herman a glare that practically shouted, *So there!*

It was hard for Marcy not to grin at the interactions between her senior sleuths. It did prove that people didn't change all that much as they age. It was an assumption that age made people into compliant, soft-spoken individuals who never rocked the boat or told a lie. If she had ever thought that, she gave it up when she arrested her first senior citizen years ago. The man shot his wife claiming he was too old for divorce. He was, however, not too old for prison.

"What do we have?" Herman refused to give it up.

"Well, Mr. Veteran Sleuth..." Lola started, waggling her index finger at the man. She shook it with each word. "We know that Jill is going to Ireland with her husband."

"So? How is that news? Lance already told Marcy that Makowski was emigrating."

It was right about this time Marcy should interrupt, but she was curious to see what Lola came up with. One of the tricks to gathering information was to remain silent and allow others to talk.

"We know Jill is going to Ireland."

Herman made the mistake of opening his mouth, but Lola spoke first. "Wait. By Jill's failure to be beside her husband in any of the news photos, we have established that our main suspect, the husband, is keeping the fact he remarried a secret. Wouldn't even have known if Gus hadn't taken a stroll through the public records."

"About that..." Herman interrupted.

Marcy had a suspicion of what he might say. "I checked. They *are* married."

A small huff sounded as Herman took a seat and motioned for Lola to continue.

"It's obvious by the lack of photos of Jill and her husband together on social media that it's either the woman is not taking the trips with her husband, which is telling, or he refuses to be in the photos, which is equally telling." She held up her hand to Herman, probably expecting him to interrupt before she could deliver her deduction. "It means it wasn't a love match. It wasn't a social match either, or Makowski would have made sure to get her in the news photos."

The pause gave Herman a chance to speak. "She's not a bad looking woman."

"Especially since she had work done," Lola was quick to add. "Wouldn't you think an older man would want to be seen with her?"

His brows lowered as if trying to work out the solution. "Some would. I know the rich are always trading in their wives for younger models, but there are inherent problems with younger women."

Even though it had nothing to do with the case, the inherent problems intrigued Marcy. "What type of problems?"

"First, you have to explain everything because they never lived through it. Due to being born in different eras, you have different preferences in everything from movies to music. A young woman wants to go all the time. It's a good way to bring on a heart attack. That's why most of those who marry younger women die from cardiac arrest trying to do things no one their age should try."

"Well now." Lola's lipstick-coated lips pulled up into a smile. "Glad to see you have some appreciation for older women."

"I do. Half the time, older women have no appreciation for me."

Lola had been going somewhere with the new wife being hidden, but if she conversed on the romantic preferences between mature individuals, her crime train of thought might derail. "Okay..." Marcy interjected and clapped her hands. "Finish your thought about the younger wife and her husband ignoring her."

"Let's go with the assumption..." Lola paused and glanced around to make sure she had everyone's attention. "...that Jill always had a crush on her boss. Unfortunately, he was married. She was always there as his Girl Friday. She knew things about him he had no clue she knew. Perhaps, he bought a gun before the murder."

As much as she hated interrupting, she felt she had to. "The weapon was not registered, but Makowski remembered his wife buying it, claiming she hadn't felt safe going to the various fundraisers all over town."

Herman grinned and shot up his hand. He spoke, remembering that he didn't have to wait to be called on. "Could we trace the gun?"

"We could." Marcy acknowledged. It was a common protocol in an actual crime. "It was never placed in evidence since it was ruled a suicide. Makes it hard to trace. Even so, it could have been a simple exchange of money for a gun, as opposed to an actual gun shop."

The chair rattled as Lola pushed to a standing position and reached for her walker. "Might as well leave if I can't even finish my theory."

"Go on..." Marcy urged, thinking seniors were every bit as prideful and territorial as beat cops.

Lola audibly inhaled, then allowed her shoulders to relax as she used a nearby chair to steady herself. "My theory is that Jill has something on her husband. There's no real love between them at this time. There may have been in the past. He spends money on her, considering the enhancements and vacations. If things were bad between them, you'd think they'd divorce, but Makowski can't take a chance on Jill spilling all she knows."

It was a workable theory. "So, do you have a plan on how to separate Jill from the goose that's laying all types of golden eggs?"

"I do. We need to offer her a more favorable goose. I have a plan to do just that. I saw it on a television show once. The show was named after a fish, I believe."

Herman sucked in his lips, then released them. "I'm willing to offer myself up as the more attractive goose." He smoothed his hand over his thick silver crown of hair.

"Thanks." Lola acknowledged his offer with a head bob. "I had someone, or should I say something, different in mind."

Chapter Twenty-Three

EXCITED VOICES CAME from the dining room, indicating something was going on. The pizza had already been delivered and destroyed in a matter of minutes. Anyone who thought older folks didn't like pizza should have witnessed the consumption of the dozens of pizzas from various parlors. Herman stuck his hands in his pockets and hunched his shoulders forward. Gwen, his grand-niece, joked it was his turtle posture. She added something about he did it when he wanted to shut everyone out.

In this case, he seemed to be the one shutout. He was the only person who had real crime-solving experience, with the notable exception of Marcy, and what was he doing? Nothing. Jake and Lola were busy cooking something up on the computer. Marcy oversaw everything and was the liaison with the local police force. Gus might not be doing all that much on the case, but he kept busy with Eunice, protesting the disaster their dietary services had become. Somehow, Gus had even managed to get them pizza delivered. He could understand the administration giving in to make Eunice go away—most people would. There was something about the woman that made people throw up their hands in surrender.

Too bad they couldn't harness that energy. Gus popped out of the dining room and waved at Herman.

"With a face that long, you should be pulling a cart."

Not what he wanted to hear. He kept walking, hoping that Gus would return to whatever he'd been doing. It would take him about twenty-two steps to make it to his room from here. The fact he had counted the number of steps to his room from each central location screamed pathetic. Gus fell into step with Herman.

"What's wrong?"

"Don't want to talk about it." That should have been enough to send an average person on their way, but not Gus.

"I bet I can guess what's wrong."

"No, you can't."

"Yes, I can."

He was ready for another refusal that Gus didn't know, but changed his mind. "Okay, Mr.-Know-It-All. What's wrong?"

"You're being shut out of the crime investigation. Sure, you drive people places since you're the only one with a car here, but no one listens to you."

Herman jingled the change in his pocket to keep from answering but managed an affirmative grunt.

"Me, too. That's part of the reason I started doing stuff with Eunice. She thinks I have something to contribute. As two of the smartest guys on the crime-solving team, we should not be shut *out*." He raised his voice on the last word and stomped his foot. "I even figured out a way not only to get back into the game but to come out a winner, too."

Even though Gus had a reputation for hare-brained schemes, the possibility he had something cooked up still tempted Herman. "What did you have in mind?"

Gus looked over his shoulder. "Not sure if we should say anything. Your room or mine?"

"Better be mine. At least that way, Eunice won't be popping out from any of the furniture because she was just in the area."

"Ha ha." He wrinkled his nose and added, "She's not that bad. The woman *is* driven. Got to give her credit that she gets done what she sets her mind on. Just like when she hid in the car when we went to North Carolina. Ha ha!"

Who was this man? He shot his friend a bewildered look. "I seem to remember you referring to her as an interfering old bat."

"Sounds like me." He waggled his eyebrows. "I didn't know then that interfering equaled driven. Sometimes, you need that type of person on your team. Reminds me of a snapping turtle." He elbowed Herman. "You know what they say about a snapping turtle."

He didn't. "I suppose you're going to tell me."

Gus hooted. "You're a treat. Certainly, glad we got you to move up here. You're much more fun to have around than Jake, especially since he's gone all secretive of late."

"The turtle?" Herman prompted. His lips lifted a little considering that at least someone was happy he was here. Then again, Gus might just be looking for someone to be the butt of his jokes. His smile slipped, then vanished altogether.

"What's up with you? A snapping turtle didn't grab ahold of your big toe. They say when a snapping turtle latches on to something or someone, it won't let go until lightning strikes it. Of course, if you're attached to the turtle when lightning struck it, then that's all she wrote."

"I don't think we have to worry about turtles." He gave a slight nod as two female residents passed on his right. The women giggled, and he would have sworn one batted her eyelashes. Herman halfway pivoted, just to make sure. Gus's hand landed on his arm and squeezed.

"Play it cool. Don't go making Loretta think you'll be had by a sultry look."

"Was that what that was?"

"Focus!"

"On what?" Herman shook off Gus's hand and turned only to find an empty corridor. "Turtles?"

"Not sure they'll be a problem. I kinda figured the country club people tried to keep the place safe. Even if a ball went into the water, no one ever bothers to fish it out. They lie about how far they drove the ball and then put another one on the green."

Here he moved to the home in a last-ditch attempt to not die alone. He sighed as he considered the vanished women. He didn't know what he would have done or said anyway, especially considering he had no clue Loretta had even existed until just now.

"Not sure why you decided to talk about golf. Never knew you to be a big player. Can't even recall you ever mentioning it until now. Still, you had plenty of time to pick up the sport."

"Not a word more until we're in your room."

"Okay." Sometimes he wondered if Gus had all his faculties. He fingered the change in his pocket trying to find his room key. Those who were residents, as opposed to being a patient, could lock their doors. Since he'd been accustomed to doing so he kept up the habit. He fished out the key, unlocked the door, and pushed it open.

Gus hurried inside and clicked on the television. He scrolled through the channels until he found a cartoon complete with squeals, blasts, and other comic sounds.

"You didn't come here to watch that show." He motioned to the television.

"What?" Gus held his hand up to his ear.

"The television show!" Herman raised his voice.

"Can't hear you!"

"Oh for Pete's sake." He grabbed the remote and turned off the television. "Can you hear me now?"

"Yes..." Gus answered and held out his hand for the remote. "With the television on, no one else could hear us. No eavesdroppers."

It was safe to assume there wouldn't be anyone outside his door listening for tidbits of information. "True, but you can't hear me. If we yell everything to be heard over the television, it beats the point of trying to be secretive. I imagine everyone would know our business. Trust me. No one is spying on us. Say what you got to say."

Gus held his finger to his lips, tiptoed to the door, opened it slowly, and stuck his head out. Satisfied, he brought it back in and closed the door. "The coast is clear, but I need to be fast. I have a friend at the country club who can get us in tomorrow."

"A member? The golf pro?"

"Better." Gus rubbed his hands together. "The Groundskeeper. We'll have to dress like golfers. He'll get us a cart and some clubs."

"We're doing this why?"

"To eavesdrop of course. The mayor and his cronies always play there, and it got me thinking. I called up Emmett, my friend, and asked him if Todd Makowski played there. He told me he always plays on Thursday morning with..." Gus paused for dramatic effect then continued, "...the former police chief."

"You think by lurking nearby we can hear a confession?"

"We'll be doing more than lurking."

Herman squeezed his eyes shut. Here it comes. The craziness he was trying to avoid. "Should I ask?"

"You should. We're going to bug the cart. A while back I ordered a listening device from a spy shop online. Tried it out in the staff lounge. The sad fact is we have more interesting lives than the staff does. All we need to do is attach it to their cart."

"That should be no problem. I'm sure a former law enforcement officer wouldn't mind being recorded." He kept his voice deadpan, waiting to see when Gus might pick up on the sarcasm.

"Yeah. I thought so, too. If that doesn't work there's always Plan B."

Could there actually be something slightly foolhardier? "Plan B?"

"Don't worry about it. Concentrate on putting together some golfing clothes. Think Arnold Palmer."

Chapter Twenty-Four

"**O**OH! HE'S HANDSOME!" Lola exclaimed, as an image of a young, blond, smiling man filled up the computer screen.

"He's not so great..." Jake grumbled from his position beside Lola. "Looks like a phony to me. Probably had all his teeth capped."

Marcy leaned forward to point at the image that caused such varying opinions. "He won't do. He's an actor, a popular one. We need a photo or photos that won't make Jill suspect she's being catfished."

"You're right." Lola made an audible exhale and started typing on the keyboard. "I found that men's hairstyle websites are a good place to find an unknown handsome man."

"Sounds like you've done this before." Jake shot her a look.

She had, but Lola didn't want to admit it. "Maybe. Let's leave it at that."

A series of images came up in small thumbnails. Marcy leaned forward to peer at them. "Nope. Too handsome. Ooh! That one looks scary—a definite no. Who would reply to a man who looked like a poster child for a serial killer?" She held up her hand. "Don't answer. I know serial killer groupies."

Lola turned to Jake, who shrugged. Here she thought she'd seen it all, but apparently, her slice of life wasn't as seedy as she had presumed. Marcy continued to reject several of the images, which would leave them with very few options. "You're knocking off all the super good-looking guys."

"That's right, I am. We want Jill to think her new guy is accessible as opposed to a group of people throwing up a photo and a fake profile. Too many people think they can put up a single photo, then compose some glamorous profile with the guy being a billionaire who jets around the world with his adorable pug doing philanthropic deeds."

It was almost like the woman had read her fake profile. "What's wrong with that?"

"Everything."

That answered nothing.

Jake chimed in. "A dude like that would have hot and cold running women. He certainly wouldn't have to find females on the Internet."

Marcy nodded. "There is that. The first giveaway is traveling with your pet. Most countries have you quarantine your pet due to mad cow disease. As much as I like to think of a billionaire doing good deeds, most of them are billionaires because they attend to business. The final giveaway is the lack of photos. Some people try to get around this by showing images of where the man traveled to but eventually the perp gets suspicious. The police have used social media to catch pedophiles and other assorted criminals all the time. The pedophiles are looking for children, which the officer pretends to be, while the other perps are looking to brag about a recent crime to impress an online romantic prospect. For reasons I haven't figured out yet, people assume they're anonymous on the Internet."

"They're not!" She assumed no one could trace *Robert Golden* back to her. Images of whatever official came to arrest you, possibly in dark suits walking the main sidewalk of the center, crowded her mind. Her voice grew tight as she asked, "How do they discover who it is?"

"We have a forensic computer specialist who can trace back the URLs. Most who make a living at defrauding people online usually do it from other countries. A woman thinks she's helping out some sexy soldier who can't get home by sending money to an online account, only to have those funds go overseas."

"Hey!" Jake waved his hands as he spoke. "Everyone knows Uncle Sam pays for a soldier to get back home. If it's a family emergency the USO can help, too."

Marcy turned her head to address Jake. "You know that because you've served. Most don't know, which is why the stranded soldier is such a successful con. We can usually bust those by looking at their social media friends. We don't even have to call in the specialist."

There's something Lola hadn't thought of. When she decided to make her profile, she decided Robert needed friends and ended up making five fake accounts for friends. "Ah, how do you do that?"

"Usually scam artists retain the same set of friends even though they're changing their names regularly. These friends are scattered across the globe and have never met the perp."

"That's good. What I meant is, it's good you caught them." At least she gave Robert Golden friends that lived close by. Marcy pinned her with an odd look as if she suspected.

She always assumed if she was going to be arrested it would have been in her much younger years. She threw her hands up. "All right. You got me. I made up a fake dating profile to see how women would respond. I guess I wanted an inside look at the competition. What I found wasn't pretty." She clicked her tongue. "What am I charged with?"

"Did you ask any for money?"

"No."

"Perform any criminal acts?"

"Of course not."

Marcy cocked her head to one side and placed her finger on her cheek. "I'm afraid I will have to charge you with being ingenious. Not sure why I never thought of doing likewise."

The three of them laughed. Jake gave her a curious glance. "Did you get many replies?"

"Hundreds. It was disheartening that so many women could be easily tricked. I wasn't even clever like Marcy is being by not making the man too handsome or too rich."

"Not surprising," Marcy added as she reached for the keyboard. "I got another website we might visit. Stock images. You have to pay a few bucks, but you can get several images of one person. Usually, they have the same clothes on, but not always. As for the women replying to your profile, too many women put a lot of faith in the Cinderella tale. Most are just waiting for their imaginary prince to show up."

It took another twenty minutes to complete the profile. Their guy, Brand—Jake insisted the name sound alpha—lived nearby, but not in the city, which would prevent Jill from doing a lookup. Just to be safe, they created another profile on a job-related media site just in case Jill wasn't willing to believe all and went looking.

"This is really easy to do." Jake shook his head and appeared bemused. "Almost too easy. What stops people from making fake profiles?"

"Almost nothing." Marcy arched her brows and smiled at Lola. "For a while, many of the profiles were coming from prisoners who had computer privileges. Those websites have since been blocked. I'm sure a computer savvy prisoner could find his way around the firewalls, though."

"Okay." Lola inhaled deeply as she thought out her plan. "We got a good profile but how can we get the two to meet? There's no time to put it on a dating site and there should be no reason Jill would be on one."

"I already thought of that." She placed her fingertips together. "Jill assumes you're a young showgirl. First, we have you befriend Brand, then gush about him in your next message. Even ask her to take a look at him."

"What if she doesn't?" Jake asked. "She doesn't want to do anything to ruin her marriage."

Both women shot him a disbelieving look while Marcy chose to verbalize her feelings. "Jake, she's only taking a look. Something you do every day."

"I'm not married."

"True. Would you go blind if you were married?"

"I guess not."

It was easy to see what point Marcy was getting at. Human nature usually had women noticing handsome men. Even she had married friends point out attractive men to her as if she missed seeing them somehow. "Besides, Jill has already demonstrated that she doesn't use the best judgment. She has an open profile that anyone can see. I suspect her husband is clueless. She's also flashing the missing blue diamond online."

Jake held up a finger. "The husband never reported it missing."

He had a point which didn't fit in with the scenario Lola had worked out in her mind. "The housekeeper noticed it was missing. Besides, if it was murder or suicide, no one says let's take off all my jewelry before I do this. Sue Ellen had bequeathed the ring to the rescue society."

"That must have burned, considering Makowski bought her the

ring."

This was a subject Lola was intimately familiar with because of her time around the gaming table when both men and women would add wedding and engagement rings to their pile of chips to up the ante. "The engagement ring is a gift, which means it belonged to Sue Ellen as soon as it was slipped onto her finger. She had the right to do whatever she wanted with it. What woman would want another woman's engagement ring?"

"A greedy one..." Jake commented.

Marcy tapped her temple. "If we had a profiler assigned to this case, she might attribute Jill's online ring photo to a desire to exert control. After all, she continues to live in Sue Ellen's shadow."

Greedy and controlling were both possibilities. "It makes me wonder why she even stays married."

Jake coughed, then cleared his throat. "Seriously? All she does is go on vacation, visit spas, and go on shopping sprees. Isn't that the life every woman wants?"

Really? That's how he thought of women. No wonder he wasn't married. Before Lola could say anything, Marcy did.

"Of all the misogynist remarks I've heard in my life, and I've heard plenty, that one is up there. I imagine there are some women who think they'd like that life until they marry into it. That also explains why many young trophy wives end up trying to break their prenups. All the things you mentioned can be fun, but they become meaningless without that special companion. All travel sites recommend women going on solo vacations. I tried it once. I just felt pathetic walking on the beach alone. As a cop, I also felt like a crime statistic waiting to happen. A single female tourist shouts opportunistic crime. No way would I be able to enjoy that lifestyle."

"You think so?" He scrubbed a hand over his face. "Maybe I

should have tried harder." He took an audible breath. "Let's get Brand out there in front of Jill and see what happens."

"Let's," Lola agreed.

They'd sent the message to Jill and were ready to leave when the activity director found them.

"There you are. We need to talk about the dance."

Chapter Twenty-Five

HERMAN SMOOTHED THE argyle sock over his calf. Thank goodness he had the appropriate socks for golf. The socks had been a gift from his former neighbor, Donna. She'd been kind enough to invite him to her Christmas festivities and always had a gift or two for him. The socks were a bit wilder than he normally wore, but he had smiled and murmured his thanks. No way could he have exchanged them. The news might have gotten back to Donna. In a town like Legacy, everything was an open secret. This would be the socks first showing.

He glanced back at the World Book he'd taken from the Florida room. Under golf, it had several men posing with gold clubs. A few had on knickers, others had loose pleated trousers, which they topped with buttoned-down shirts and sweater vests. A few had cardigans. One even had one of those newsboy caps. The only cap he had was a Greek fisherman's hat, which was somewhat similar. As for sweater vests, Herman never wore them, but someone had given him one at the last reunion.

That's the type of stuff you got when people didn't know you. Pajama bottoms with fruit on it, books about subjects you couldn't care less about and he suspected were on clearance, and sweater vests, which actually worked for him this time. The big question was where was it? He pawed through his hanging clothes. *Nothing.* He checked the bureau without success. Obviously, it was something he didn't wear. Maybe it was in the boxes he hadn't bothered to unpack.

He heaved a sigh of disgust and pulled out the four boxes from under his bed. After rifling through old knick-knacks, tablecloths for tables he no longer owned, and photos of people whose names he'd forgotten, he found the vest. Hooray! He pulled out the blue and yellow vest.

"Sure is bright." Golf was a game, so it followed that the clothes would be playful. He placed the vest on the bed and went in search of a coordinating shirt. He took a few minutes to tweak his clothes to his satisfaction. The vest was a tad more flamboyant than he liked, but the photo in the World Book was in black and white. It could mean that the golfers had on vivid colors like pink or yellow.

A rat-tat, tatty, tat, tat knock sounded on his door. It was the agreed-upon secret code Gus had insisted on using. It had to be Gus or a determined Avon Lady. He swung the door open to see Gus attired in slacks and a pullover sweater. Obviously, the man did not get the memo about golf apparel.

"Is that what you're wearing?" Gus had the nerve to ask.

"Of course it is." *Typical.* Just like the man to fuss about his clothes when he hadn't taken time with his own wardrobe. "I researched my outfit, which is more than I can say about yours."

"Ha!" Gus gave Herman's outfit a thorough perusal. "Did your research include watching the Three Stooges?"

"No. I used the World Book."

"1927 edition?"

"You're so funny, I forgot to laugh." He strolled over to pick up the World Book he'd been using as a reference. He placed his finger on the page, to not lose the image of the golfers and flipped back to find the copyright date. "It's not 1927, it's—1947."

"Oh, good, after the War. Things have changed some." Gus pointed to Herman's rolled up pants. "Would you please fix your pants."

"These knickers are the best I could approximate. I'll roll them down," He held up his hand and met his friend's eyes with a direct stare. "Only because they wouldn't stay when I started to move around, not because you told me to."

"Yeah, right. There isn't that much of a dress guideline for golf players. Emmett told me no jeans. Since jeans imply you could be an ordinary person. No T-shirts for the same reason. You might want cleats, but I suspect since we'll be doing very little golfing, we can get by with loafers. You might want to ditch the rubber duckie vest."

Rubber duckies? He stepped over to the full-length mirror attached to his closet door. The yellow spots were rubber ducks. Here he thought it was some abstract design. He could change, but it would amuse Gus too much. Instead, he shook out his pant legs until they broke across his loafers. "Let's go."

"Let me grab my listening device. I couldn't find the small one. I have to resort to the old parabolic microphone and cassette player."

Gus stepped out of the room and picked up a box big enough for a circular sander. For a second, Herman was relieved that neither he nor Gus would have to sneak up to Makowski's golf cart and plant a listening device. Whatever was in that oversized box would not be subtle. Part of him wanted to call off the plan. Since there was no alternative, he stepped into the hall and locked his door. They turned and headed for the H unit. No one had to tell him twice the appropriate way to exit with the least amount of hassle. Gus nudged him.

"Put your shoulders back, chin up, act like you know what you're doing, and no one will question you."

Unlike Gus, he could come and go as he pleased. His friend smiled at staff members and wished them a good day.

When they got outside, he asked, "What was all that good day nonsense about? I thought the idea was not to attract attention."

"To an extent." Gus held his hand vertical and tipped it slightly. "We need to look casual, not guilty or covert. Besides, I needed to balance out your duck sweater, which shouts senility."

He aimed a playful punch at Gus's shoulder that the man dodged with a quick sidestep. "Just be glad you are one of my few remaining friends."

"I know. You're probably the only one of my friends who can take a joke."

Herman harrumphed to himself, not all that certain he could take a joke. They reached the car and headed out using Gus's faded remembrance of where the country club used to be. An upscale subdivision was there now and sported the name Country Club Estates. They did locate a friendly resident that directed them to the new location, which was built almost twenty years ago.

Once on the grounds, Herman parked near a landscaping shed, where a man in an off-green shirt and pants came out to meet them. Gus waved and commented. "That's Emmett. You need to give him a twenty."

"What?" There was no mention of this before they left.

"It's for the cart. I have to give him a twenty, too."

That made sense. Once the money exchanged hands and Emmett made a big show of winking at them, crossing his heart, and swearing he'd never seen them, he guided them to a golf cart loaded with two golf bags.

Gus looked back in the direction of the parking lot. "I forgot my box."

While his friend jogged back to the car, Herman took time to question Emmett. "Has Makowski arrived yet?"

"He and the former police chief aren't that far ahead. Neither one is that great of a golfer. That's why they try to pick that sweet time when there aren't too many golfers on the course. They can take as many mulligans as they need."

"Got it." Herman climbed into the cart to drive before Gus arrived. With his friend's extra zealousness in the venture, the man might end up rear-ending the other golf cart. It had been a while since he'd been in a golf cart, but it worked the same as the others. He took it for a small jaunt, testing out the turning radius. He could see Gus running for all he was worth.

"Herman, wait!"

Even though he planned to wait on his friend, he goosed the car the tiniest bit to be funny and almost hit another cart veering back onto the path. The red-faced man hit the horn that emitted a high-pitched squeak. Herman pulled the steering to the right to get out of the way. The driver glared at him while a male passenger sat looking straight ahead, reminding him of a zombie. Gwen was always talking about a zombie apocalypse. Looks like the man was already a victim. Although there was something familiar about him.

Gus caught up with the cart, lumbered into it, collapsed back into his seat with a giant exhale. He motioned for Herman to go on as he caught his breath. The cart climbed a small hill with some effort. As they crested the slope, he could see the two men he almost hit talking with barely a foot between them.

"There's our suspect. Probably telling his friend why he needs to leave the country," Gus explained as he pulled something out of the box that had a type of clear plastic dish on it. The box was stowed in the back with the clubs. "Okay, let me turn this on."

"Turn what on? Looks like you have the death ray from the Buck Rogers movies."

Gus held out the instrument. "Now that you mention it, it does."

The sound of two men's voices sounded in the cart. Herman peered behind him. No one there. There was the sound of static as Gus held out his arm, pointing it toward the two conversing men.

"I wish you weren't leaving, Todd. Anyone else I might play golf with will expect a straightforward game with no mulligans."

"It's the right thing to do."

"It's Jill. I know it is. It was a mistake to marry so fast after Sue Ellen's suicide. You were still in the grieving stage."

"I know. I regret my rush."

"Haven't you heard of divorce? I've done it three times myself. It can be expensive, but it isn't impossible."

"I've considered it. In this country, Jill would take me to the cleaners, and then some."

A hoarse laugh sounded. "I understand. I bet you'll check out the divorce laws in Ireland."

"Something like that."

Gus turned to Herman. "Did you hear that? He's going to get rid of his second wife, too."

Before either could speculate, one of the men turned to reach for a golf club. "What is that old geezer in the cart pointing at us?"

It didn't take any major brain power to figure out who was the old geezer. Herman turned the cart in a tight circle and floored it. They bumped along at about ten miles an hour. In his younger days, he could have easily caught up with the cart. The last thing he needed was to be caught doing something that appeared suspicious. It might be hard to convince a former police chief that people in a public place should be expected to be overheard, especially elected officials.

"Gus, what are they doing?"

"Let me aim this thing and maybe I can hear."

"Use your eyes, man! Are they getting into their cart or running?"

A sideways glance revealed his friend fiddling with his device and twisting in his seat to point it at him. Voices soon illuminated him about the nature of the situation.

"Come on, Todd, forget the clubs. We'll come back for them. You have your name engraved on the staffs. Everyone knows they're yours. We got to get after these guys. The one with the duck vest on almost rammed us."

"Who do you think they are? Investigative reporters?"

"Don't make me laugh."

"Private eyes?" It almost sounded like there was a tremor in the man's voice, but that could be due to bumping along the path in a golf cart.

Gus pointed across a grassy expanse with a few flags waving. "Cut across! They're gaining on us."

While no golfer, Herman was almost sure there was some rule about driving across the grass. If Makowski didn't get them, surely the groundskeeper would. A golf ball bounced off the side of the cart. "Good gravy! They must have some bad golfers out here."

Gus didn't say a word but clutched his parabolic mic and stared straight ahead.

Another golf ball knocked Herman's Greek fisherman hat off. "What's going on? Is there a convention of Bad Golfers Anonymous?"

Gus peeked behind them. "Good news is they aren't following us."

That was good news. A ball grazed his knuckles, causing him to take one hand off the wheel. "That stung."

"Bad news is we drove onto the driving range, which is probably why they aren't following us."

A quick glance to his right revealed a few golfers swinging madly at the balls with what looked like absolute determination to try to hit them. "Gus, are you trying to get us killed?"

"Head to the equipment shed. We'll lose the cart. You need to ditch the sweater vest. With any luck, we'll be near a restaurant, or a bar, or someplace to hide."

They made it to the concrete building with a few ball-shaped bruises for their efforts and a cracked dish on the parabolic mic. They stopped the cart behind the building. Herman shed his sweater vest in a nearby trash can. His hat lay somewhere on the driving range.

Gus gave a sorrowful look at the broken mic. "Goodbye. Good spy equipment is hard to come by." Then he tossed it in the can. He ran his fingers through his hair and pulled it into clumps. "I'm working on my disguise. The fact you lost the vest and hat is good. Untuck the shirt for a more casual look."

They strolled back slowly to the car, spotting Emmett on the way. They explained where they'd left the golf cart.

"I guessed as much when I heard the yelling. I hope you got what you wanted."

About all they knew was that Makowski didn't want to leave, but felt he had to. The implication was Jill had something to do with it. Gus grabbed the groundskeeper's hand and shook it hard. "Had a great time. Made me feel young again."

Chapter Twenty-Six

MARCY WIPED AWAY a tear due to laughing as Gus re-enacted their adventures on the golf course. She should scold him for even trying such an adventure, but he appeared to enjoy it so much, and no harm was done except for a few golf ball bruises. "You think the chief recognized you?"

Herman answered with a shake of his head. "He was looking for a guy with a yellow duck sweater vest and a Greek fisherman cap. I lost both out on the driving range."

"How did you lose them?"

"Don't ask. Unlike Gus, I'd prefer to forget the entire incident."

She held up an index finger. "Before you do, tell me what you learned."

"It was odd. It seemed obvious the chief and Makowski are good friends. The chief didn't want him to leave. Makowski insisted he didn't want to but had to because of Jill."

"Why doesn't he just divorce her?" It seemed like the obvious solution to her.

Herman bobbed his head in agreement. "Chief asked that, too. Makowski talked about not being able to do that, but he had something planned."

That in itself sounded suspicious. "Ireland seems like an unlikely choice. If it's a divorce he wants, he'll have to wait a year to become a resident. If he fears extradition, he'd be better off going to Brazil.

Ireland has its wild areas and islands. It might be easy for someone to vanish if that was his intention."

"He insisted he didn't want to go."

"That could be for show."

Lola, who was seated nearby, switched her attention from Gus's antics to the conversation. "Jill insists she doesn't want to go to Ireland. When you consider all her photos of the various exotic ports she's been to, I believe her. Maybe this trip is a smokescreen. They both go their separate ways. It looks like they're going to Ireland, but they vanish to parts unknown."

Gus dropped in a chair leaving Jake free to migrate to their corner. "I think you all are forgetting about Mabel. Sure, she left. Could be she went ahead to Ireland. Maybe she felt we were snooping around and exited the scene. Leaving her stuff would make us think she was coming back."

"Where could she go?" Marcy wondered aloud, knowing the possibilities were endless with enough money.

"Anywhere." Jake pointed out the obvious. "Is your friend Lance watching the bus stations, the airport, or any other way Mabel could leave town?"

"No." She pursed her lips, thinking how easy it would be for Mabel to vanish. Still, if the woman was guilty, why would she stay around? Jill's social media photos demonstrated that Mabel didn't have the diamond. Mentally, she walked through the timeline. Mabel found the body. She called the police and the husband. She would have commented on the missing ring if it had been missing when she found the body. No insurance claims have been filed on the sizable ring. It was obvious Jill had it now. The common assumption was her husband removed it from his wife's cold, dead finger, after he killed her, but what if he didn't? "Have you heard anything back on the Brand profile?"

"I'll need to check," Lola volunteered and snuck a look at Jake.

He held up his hands, waving them back and forth. "We can't ask Katie to use her office again. I don't want to risk getting her in trouble. Gus has a computer."

The four of them turned hopeful eyes on Gus who had his eyes closed, his mouth slightly ajar, snoring softly.

"Oh come on!" Jake jostled the man. "I know you're not asleep. You were more of a whistler when you snored."

Gus opened his eyes. "At least I didn't sound like a 747 taking off like you do. I'll let you use my computer. Don't make a habit of it, though. I thought Katie was bringing us a computer."

"She is. I hate to bug her about it since she's having trouble with her ex right now. He's not paying support, and it's hard to take care of the kids with what she makes here."

"I understand. I guess you can use my laptop as long as you need it." Gus turned to stare at Marcy. "I'm surprised you don't have a computer."

"I did. It was considered the department's property. Since I am on medical leave, it was taken back, and possibly allotted for someone else to use. I agree I need a computer. The tablet I have isn't much good except for reading emails and playing a few games. Maybe we can make a shopping run in the near future."

Herman smiled. "You bet."

She pointed to Gus. "Go get your computer. Try not to be way-laid by Eunice."

"Aye, I will." He gave her a crisp salute and headed out.

She had hoped this unique band of seniors would help her recall forgotten buildings or street names that had been changed. What she didn't expect was the unique perspectives or feisty attitudes. "I have a feeling that we're close, very close. I need to call Lance. Needless to say, when an individual feels cornered is when he's the most dangerous."

Even though she had their attention, it didn't seem as if her message was getting through. They all smiled back and nodded as if she was talking about the book of the month or a change in the bingo schedule.

She inhaled and decided to start again. "I'm grateful for all that you have done, but it could prove too dangerous to go any further."

Jake pounded his fist into his hand. "It's not in my nature to let a killer roam free."

This was what she didn't want. The last thing she needed was for someone to get hurt.

Lola cleared her throat. "I get it. We aren't going to run anyone down, especially me, but we *can* serve as support."

"That's right." She gestured to her own chair. "The best I could do is roll into someone and knock them down. We'll get the details and pass them on to Lance."

"Got it." Gus entered the room and brandished his white laptop.

"Any trouble with Eunice?" Herman inquired.

"None I couldn't handle. Thank goodness I don't have your height since I hid behind those potted plants in the lobby area until Eunice left." He shook his head. "I know she can be a bit too much, but that woman is a demon on details. Remember Jake, you said something about hearing the dietary director saying something about how much money she's saving by changing up the menu?"

"I did."

"Eunice has made up spreadsheets about what we used to be served compared to what we are currently being served and the estimated price differences. The prices are retail and estimated since she doesn't have access to wholesale. She took a bit of information and ran with it."

"It's impressive." Marcy agreed. "Right now isn't a good time to bring someone new into the group."

Gus cleared his throat. "I wasn't asking you to. I just felt that sometimes everyone thinks the worst of Eunice. She'd work hard if you give her a task. Trust me. We wouldn't have had pizza if it wasn't for Eunice."

"I believe you. Let's get that computer fired up and see how Jill has responded to Lola's request to check out Brand."

It took a few minutes for the older computer to boot up. A few keystrokes got them where they needed to go. The five of them hovering around the computer made it rather difficult to see. "Could someone turn on the lights?"

The overhead light flickered to life, throwing a yellow glow over the group and making it a bit easier to see. "Click on Brand's profile."

Gus did as asked. "Look here. I think Brand has mail."

"Yes!" Marcy clapped her hands together. "Let's see what it is."

Gus clicked on the message. "Whoo-whee! It's a friend invite."

"Not surprised." Lola clicked her tongue. "The woman is starved for attention."

"Where do we go from here?" Herman asked the most obvious question.

"You go nowhere. With any luck, we can arrange a meeting between Jill and Brand."

Jake arched his eyebrows and tilted up his chin. "I think I could pass for Brand in the right lighting."

Lola gave a heavy sigh. "You're a handsome man, but you're a mature man. Jill will be expecting some young guy."

"Exactly. I'm sure Lance can find some beat cop that looks enough like Brand for her not to question it too much. With Photoshop, everyone enhances their photos. When we get right down to it, Jill might not bear too much resemblance to her photos, either. Right now, we need to get them talking. You might come in handy, Jake. The word around the center is you have a smooth banter."

Gus sat up and grinned. "Yeah, the other soldiers used to say he could talk a woman out of her unmentionables." His face flushed. "Ah, pardon me. Present company excluded, of course."

Marcy chose not to say anything. Instead, she gestured to the table where Gus placed the computer, and Marcy rolled up to it. "I'm not sure how long our conversation will be. If Jill is as lonesome as Lola suspects she is, it could be hours."

Lola crossed her arms. "I'm staying."

"Me, too." Herman offered.

"Since I am the purveyor of romantic messages, I have to stay," Jake announced with a smirk.

"That may be," Gus added with a nod. "I'm the substitute when you run dry, and you will."

"What makes you think that?"

Gus sauntered over to Jake and slapped him on the back. "You forget. I was married for thirty years. I know what to say to woman three hundred-sixty-five days a year. It takes more work coming up with new sweet nothings than to keep recycling the same ones."

The conversation started and went long, almost three hours until finally, Marcy pushed for a meeting as Brand. She suggested a dark, intimate restaurant that might not display too badly how Brand didn't look like his picture. All she had to do was pass the information to Lance, but something still didn't feel right.

Chapter Twenty-Seven

THE PLAN WAS for a rather hunky-looking—Lola's word, not his—patrolman to play the part of Brand. He'd show up wearing a wire at the restaurant and over a couple of drinks, Jill would reveal that her husband was a murderer. Herman didn't think this was likely. Sure, he hadn't been in the dating world for possibly centuries, but there were two things wrong with the scenario. A woman using the words *murder* and *husband* would definitely put a damper on a first date.

Although Marcy explained she probably wouldn't say exactly that, Jill might drop hints about knowing something of the sensational nature, just to look important. While that sounded more realistic, it still seemed a little farfetched. After they did all the work, some unknown flat foot could possibly sew up their case. It didn't seem right.

He was on his way to Marcy's room to see if she'd heard anything yet. Herman could have called, but he could use the exercise and an excuse to get out of his room. A man in his unit was authorized to get a therapy dog. Not sure exactly why he needed a therapy dog since he could see just fine. However, it gave the dog owner a chance to go outside and walk his dog every day, which was fine during nice weather, but probably not too fun in the winter. Still, it might give the man purpose, which is what the crime solving group did for him.

Once this case was solved, there could be another. That would depend on the case being solved, though. Lola had decided the killer was a woman, and it had something to do with the ring. It was obvious Makowski knew exactly where the ring had been, or Jill wouldn't have it.

His footsteps stopped as he considered the possibility that the Brand wannabe might be meeting with a murderess. If so, why would she have anything against Brand? All he knew was she was lonely, unhappy, and looking for a change. That could describe a good portion of the population.

"Herman! Yoo-hoo!" He smiled as he pivoted, expecting Loretta. *Eunice.* He should have known. Her voice sounded different. Friendly, as opposed to her usual demanding tone. His momentary pause turned him into a sitting duck. *Now what?* Where was Gus when you needed him?

"Ah, Eunice." He greeted her because to do otherwise would have been rude. His knees wouldn't cooperate with him, either, attempting a mad dash down the hall. There wasn't a lot of things he could claim, but he had been brought up in a time where men had to be polite to women, no matter what.

"Great! I caught up with you. I was on my way to see Marcy."

"Why?" There was no need unless she wanted to badger the woman about their made-up gardening club or possibly the dance the activities director put down for November. She'd decided some might find Halloween an inappropriate time, although he could see it working. Many organizations visited during December, they didn't need one more social event.

"Something peculiar happened when I was sitting out on the front porch."

He knew it probably involved gossip about one of the residents stealing a kiss or sneaking a smoke. "Okay. Who'd you catch smoking this time?"

"I spotted Jake. He had one of those vape things that all the kids have nowadays. They come in all sorts of cookie and food flavors."

"Jake? Vape?" That explained his secretiveness and why the man had started smelling like a bakery.

"Yeah," Eunice answered and gave him a poke with her pointed nail. "That wasn't the weird thing. I need to get to Marcy's room before that woman does, and I'm wasting time talking to you." She picked up her pace, moving fast for a small woman.

Herman had to stretch out his gait to keep up. "What woman?"

Eunice had fisted her hands and was swinging them in a race walk fashion as she sped along. "A middle-aged woman told me she was Marcy's sister and asked for her room number."

"Marcy doesn't have a sister. At least, she never mentioned one."

"I wondered why a sister would just show up now?" Eunice pointed down the hall. "That's her!"

There was only a flash of a woman turning the corner in a trench coat and sunglasses, but he knew it was Mabel. What if they were all wrong? The only person who knew for sure they were investigating Sue Ellen's death was Mabel. She could have been the culprit. She had access, or maybe she was here to silence Marcy on behalf of her lover. "We've got to stop her."

"I know!" Eunice managed to move faster, but a stitch in Herman's side was making it hard to move at all.

Body, don't fail me now. Marcy's life might depend on it. He tried to convince himself the woman might want to share information, but the fist twisting his gut said otherwise. Off to the side, he spotted the new scooter one of the residents had bragged about. Said it went up to thirty miles per hour to be used on the street. It was probably an exaggeration. Whatever it was had to be faster than what he was doing.

The keys were in the ignition, which served him well. Herman floored it and heard someone yell. "Thief!"

Good. It would get the staff riled up. He swerved around some slow-moving residents who yelled at him. He caught up with Eunice who plopped herself into the front basket.

"Good thinking, Herman."

Even though she was a small woman, Eunice still blocked his vision.

"Stop swerving. Go straight. I'll guide you."

He had his doubts about her guidance, but it was only a few more yards to Marcy's room. All he had to do was avoid the sides of the hallway where housekeeping usually parked their carts. He made it to the room and stopped. Eunice vaulted from the basket. He abandoned the scooter and entered the room only to hear Eunice shout. "Stop! Police!"

Mabel turned to check out the claim and was hit by a glass paperweight, which knocked her off balance. Marcy aimed a cane at the back of Mabel's knees, bringing down the woman and sending the gun in her hand scudding across the floor. Finally, it was his turn to leap into action. He followed the trail of the weapon, scooped it up, and held the snub-nosed pistol on the downed woman.

Voices sounded in the hallway with one outraged one that rose above the rest. "There's my scooter!"

An elderly man, still attired in his pajamas, entered the room and pointed at Herman. "There's the thief!" When he saw the gun, he scampered back into the hall. "Call the police! He has a gun!"

★

MARCY HADN'T BEEN totally convinced that Todd Makowski was the culprit. She hadn't been persuaded of Jill's guilt either, but she was certainly troubled. She'd been listening to the conversation between Brand and Jill via her phone. In it, Jill had been describing her initial attraction to her husband and how she thought he was the smartest, most wonderful man in the world. Not your usual date talk, she was waiting for the part when Jill explain how it all turned bad. She was recording it on her handheld recorder for the other crime solvers, just in case it yielded the important confession, not that she thought it would. Those who confessed wanted to be caught. If someone had wanted to confess, ten years was plenty of time to do so. By this time, a person would be congratulating themselves on the perfect crime.

Mabel showing up surprised her a little. Marcy figured the woman would have been smart enough to leave the country when she could, if guilty. Instead, the woman had charged into her room, brandishing a gun and shouting at her. She pressed the play button on her recorder to listen to the conversation.

"Why couldn't you just leave things like they were?"

"I'm not sure what you're talking about."

Marcy smiled, glad her voice sounded calm and didn't betray any of the anxiety she had been feeling at that moment.

"You and all your snoopy friends sticking your noses where they don't belong."

"I did introduce myself as a detective. Solving crimes is what I do."

"I see you're in a wheelchair. Heard about your accident on the news. I'd think you'd learn by now that some things were best left alone or at least keep with the recent crimes. Todd wasn't bothering anyone, but he's leaving because he heard someone was investigating Sue Ellen's death again."

"You told him."

"So, I did. The man had a right to know. He's been good to me. Todd felt bad about me finding the body. Then, he laid me off since he wanted to move his piece-on-the-side into the house, and he didn't want me knowing about it. Although I knew. In fact, Sue Ellen knew. That's why she changed her will and asked me to witness the change. She said if anything happens to me, be suspicious. She even bought a gun after she heard the news that a new life insurance policy had been taken out on her."

"Why didn't she call the police or even better, get a divorce?"

"She had contacted a divorce lawyer, which put me in between them. Todd is telling me one thing, she another. Finally, Sue Ellen told me she had a paste ring made of her pretentious blue diamond ring. That's what she was wearing when she died."

"How did Jill end up with it?"

"You're asking too many questions, but I'll tell you."

There was a short screech and the sound of falling, then Eunice and Herman's voices. In the background, she could hear someone yelling, "Thief!" However, Marcy still didn't know what happened to the blue diamond.

Her cell phone chimed. A glance at the number confirmed it was Lance. "What did you find out?"

"Lots."

"I thought I'd visit in person to give you the full report."

Marcy made a slight growl.

"Okay. Okay. No need to be ugly about it. Our housekeeper was on the run, and we found the blue diamond ring in her luggage, which was loaded in her car, which we finally located in the Greener Pastures parking lot, along with a ticket to the Bahamas. I told her you had her on tape confessing to the murder of Sue Ellen. She insisted it was an accident. She accidentally shot the missus, but in my opinion, she appears way too fond of Mr. Makowski. When they brought him in for questioning, he was adamant that he had no part in his wife's death."

"What about the insurance policy?"

"Supposedly, Makowski took that out since employers often take out life insurance policy on employees. It's very hard to replace valuable employees. I wonder if Sue Ellen considered herself a valuable employee?"

"Looks like he had no trouble replacing her."

"Ha! Those two are now lovey-dovey. Jill knew about the insurance policy since she opens all the business mail and suspected Makowski had killed his wife. The husband suspected his affair with his assistant would make him look guilty and worked out a deal with Jill that she could be the missus when enough time had passed. He may have been relying on outdated information that a wife can't testify against her husband."

"Yeah. That is outdated." She wrinkled her nose, realizing the premise behind it. "That was based on the assumption the husband told the wife what to do, and she did it."

"Those were the days." A sigh sounded before he continued. "Ironically, Makowski thought Jill could be the guilty party and was tying himself to a murderess. The relationship soured after that, since they both looked at each other with different eyes. There was a touching reunion in the interrogation room."

"Yuk! Glad I missed out on that. What about the ring in the social media photos?"

"It's paste. Jill admitted it was mailed to her with a note saying she should have it as the new Mrs. Makowski. She wasn't sure who sent it and never showed it to her husband, afraid he might take it back. She was holding onto it as a nest egg."

"What do you think?"

"I think Mabel sent it in an effort to stir up some suspicion between the newlyweds, thinking Jill could be nailed for the murder, but the ring wouldn't have been enough."

"I would put Mabel down for premeditated murder, since the woman is smart enough to have left no real clues, other than the fact she'd found the body."

Lance replied, "I agree. The one thing I know is we couldn't have uncovered this crime without your help. I'll have to send more cases your way."

"Send me as many cases as you want. I can handle them."

A "woo-hoo!" and some whispering sounded outside her door.

Lance asked, "Did you say something?"

"That was the wind, I believe. Keep me informed on Mabel. Don't forget to send me more cases as soon as possible."

"Will do. I'll deliver them in person. It would be great to see you when you're not threatening to beat someone with a cane."

"I only tripped her with the cane. Besides, you're the one who brought me the cane to begin with. Thank you by the way. It would have been harder to ram her with the wheelchair and would have lacked the element of surprise, too."

They murmured their goodbyes and hung up. Marcy stared at her almost closed door. "I know you're out there! Come in."

Herman, Gus, Jake, and Lola shuffled in. Lola spoke. "Was that Lance? I bet he has a crush on you."

"Please. He's my former partner. If he had a crush on me, he had plenty of time to make it known."

"Maybe," Lola's eyes twinkled as she smiled. "Absence makes the heart grow fonder."

"Out of sight, out of mind," Gus added, only to get a pinch from Lola. "That's just mean."

"You got to learn when not to speak."

Herman cleared his throat. "The reason we showed up was to follow up on our first case, which sounds like it has been resolved."

"It has. I would love to pin premeditated murder on Mabel, but I may have to settle for manslaughter, theft, and obstruction of justice. She should be looking at ten years, maybe more, depending on the judge and jury. Sue Ellen was a very well-liked citizen."

Herman continued. "Fooled me. I thought Mabel appeared normal. I did have my suspicions. In hindsight, I can see she was trying to distract us by giving us enough clues to look elsewhere. It may take a village to raise a child, but it takes all of us to solve a crime."

Gus held up a finger. "Plus one."

"What do you mean plus one?"

You never knew with Gus. Marcy had discovered the man had enough ingenuity and energy for men half his age.

"Eunice. Eunice could be a member of…" He turned to Lola. "What was the name you came up with?"

"Senior Sleuth Service." She grinned wide. "You may not want to use it since you're young."

Marcy waved away what was probably meant to be a compliment. "AARP has already been sending me invitations to join. If I can hang out with cool seniors like you, I want to be a member." Her eyes drifted to the door. "As for Eunice, how could I say no to a woman who can toss a paperweight with such deadly accuracy?"

"Hooray!" The door swung open and a beaming Eunice entered. "I'm glad. It was getting tiring following you guys everywhere. What should we do first?"

A uniformed employee poked her head in the door. "There you all are. The activity director is looking all over for you. Something about a dance committee."

Marcy acknowledged the woman with a nod. "Thank you."

She waited for the employee to leave before she signaled to Herman. "Get the car ready. We're heading out for a celebration lunch. Let's make it quick so we don't get caught. Scatter!"

The senior sleuths headed for the door in such a hurry that Jake and Herman got stuck trying to exit at the same time. They popped out with a grunt and a muttered curse and headed in their respective ways.

Marcy noticed Eunice was still standing. "Ah, I meant…"

"I know what you meant. I've been investigating suspicious goings-on before you were even born. I'm the expert at redirection, too. Get a move on and I'll engage the activity director in a discussion about inappropriate books in the library." She winked at Marcy. "See you in a minute."

Epilogue

A SMALL LED candle flickered inside a colored votive holder. Gus poked at the votive and gave a derisive sniff. "We aren't even allowed real candles."

Herman had never considered the importance of having candles. Not having a wax one mattered little to him. The music swelled into a crescendo, swallowing the rest of the rant. Couples swayed in the dimly lit dining room. Only the food area was clearly visible where several residents stood loading their plates while uniformed employees kept the chafing plates full. "At least we don't have fake food anymore."

"Calling that mess food, fake or otherwise, would be a lie. Thank goodness Jake put a bug in Katie's ear."

"Yes," Herman agreed and picked up a tiny hotdog in a crescent roll blanket. "This is much tastier, and I can actually recognize my food. Whatever happened to the previous dietary director?"

Gus brightened and sat up a little straighter, which was an odd reaction to the subject. His gaze was fixed past Herman, but he still answered. "Locked up. Being held on embezzlement. I guess you could say we solved two crimes at once. A double-header."

His voice trailed off, making Herman turn to see what had caught his friend's attention. It was just Eunice. He did a double take, because the woman wore an actual dress, but glanced away quickly to keep the keen-eyed woman from remarking on it. He could hear Gus murmuring compliments, and Eunice giggling girlishly. They vanished into the crowd, possibly hitting the dance floor. The music changed into the Bunny Hop and even those who hadn't been dancing joined the line, following the prompts from the song to hop, hop, hop and laughing as they attempted to do so. The line swung by his table with Jake bringing up the rear.

"Come on, Herman! Have some fun."

He shook his head. No way he was getting up there to make a fool of himself. The line whipped by without him. Just when he thought he was alone in the semi-darkness, a woman's voice sounded.

"Could I join you? I arrived late and all my friends must be on the dance floor."

There stood the woman, elegant in a floral chiffon dress, the same woman Gus had pointed out to him as having a crush on him. Maybe Gus was right. Herman pushed to his feet. "Allow me." He pulled out a chair with a flourish. "I'd be glad for the company."

She smiled up at him as she sat. "I'm not much for hopping around. How about you?"

This is where it got tricky. He didn't know much about dating, but he did know simple questions were often more than they seemed. Without Jake around for guidance, he'd just have to wing it. "I may be old-fashioned, but I prefer the slow dances where a man actually gets the pleasure of holding a woman in his arms."

She gave his arm a playful tap. "You're such a flirt."

No one had ever accused him of being a flirt. The possibility stretched his smile even more. "By the way, I'm Herman. I'm new here."

"I know." She gave an elegant nod. "I'm Loretta."

The Bunny Hop line ended, and the music segued into a slow

tune. Herman stood and held out his hand. "May I have this dance?"

"I was hoping you'd ask."

He took her hand, grateful that Jake had insisted he practice his rusty dance skills, and led her onto the floor. The singer crooned about a nightingale singing on Berkeley Square. They circled the room slowly. Jake leaned against the wall, talking to Lola, and gave him a thumbs up as they drifted by. On the far side of the room, Marcy sat with her head angled toward her former partner, Lance, listening to what he was saying.

All his friends were having a great time. Suddenly, Herman realized he was, too. No reason for him to go back to Legacy. He was home now.

The End

A Bark in the Night

(Book One)

Chapter One

A GROAN ESCAPED the silent watcher as the girl pulled out a bunch of keys to unlock the front door. The dog that had been sitting now silently stood, his ears alert, his head slowly swinging side to side as he emitted a low growl.

"Damn it." He hadn't counted on a dog. Who takes a dog with them to an office building anyhow? He could have knocked down the girl and grabbed the keys, and finally made it into the building. He'd spent the last six months trying to enter the place.

The few remaining offices weren't open to the public. He'd even donned delivery outfits and tried to get buzzed in. All he managed to discover was no one in the building had water delivered or even a pizza. Usually, he received no reply when he buzzed. It could be that the buzzer didn't work. The building itself was circa 1930s and only the bottom floor was stores, while the rest were apartments or offices.

That would have worked fine if there was an actual store on the first floor instead of empty rooms. He'd considered breaking in, but he'd most likely get caught and end up back in the slammer. Something he'd prefer to avoid since he had more enemies inside than he did out. Now, he'd have to rethink the situation. Once the girl and her dog entered the building, he tucked his hands into his jacket pocket to feel the short length of pipe he'd hidden there. A man had to protect himself, but as a felon, a gun would automatically earn a huge fine and possibly incarceration. Things he wanted to avoid.

Hands still in pockets, he strolled in the direction of Monument Circle. Sweat dotted his face due to the early heat wave. He could have pulled off his sweatshirt, but the hoodie provided conformity that made him almost invisible.

In the center of the city stood a huge war monument reaching toward the heavens as if trying to touch the departed or at least send a message they hadn't been forgotten. He couldn't remember when it had been built—sometime after the Civil War. As a kid, his grandfather had taken him there. With each war, more statues and flat memorials engraved with names appeared. He remembered fingering the names thinking the people only became important by dying. That wasn't going to be him. Nope, he'd had enough of being Toby Nobody. Once he got into the building, he'd find what was his by right and buy that sailboat he fantasized about while doing time. Might even sail around the world.

Foot and vehicle traffic picked up as he made his way to the circle. A horse-driven carriage, complete with picture-snapping tourists, passed him on one side. The harness bells jingled with the horse's movements. He was not sure why a person would even bell a horse. The animal was too large to miss. Then again, maybe the owner thought it made the experience more festive. Toby stopped and watched the slow-moving carriage. He'd never taken a carriage ride, never took a gondola ride down the canal, either. Nope, those things were for tourists or people with a lot of throwaway money. Soon, that would be him, as soon as he got rid of the obstacles.

NALA PLACED ONE hand on her hip and kept a tight grip on the leash clipped to a handsome black German shepherd mix as she surveyed the building. The stone façade building rose a good five stories, nothing compared to the other buildings looming behind it on a more visited street in Indianapolis. The morning sun revealed chipped parts of the façade and the crumbling entrance steps, exposing the underlying concrete block structure.

"The building has character." She glanced up and down the street, noticing the lack of foot traffic during the early day. The ground floor windows revealed empty rooms inside where light spots on the industrial gray carpet revealed where furniture once sat. "I was never shown a ground floor office or even one with wraparound windows." Her shoulders went up in a shrug. "It is just as well. Anyone visiting a private eye doesn't want to be on display. I probably couldn't afford it anyhow. Let's go see *our* office."

The dog gave a bark as if he understood. Nala's straight hair swung into her face as she bent to pat the animal. "That's right, Max. It's a new start for both of us."

Max and Nala climbed the first flight of stairs in silence. By the time they reached the second flight, a young man with a dark hipster beard and arms full of labeled boxes met them.

"Hey, a dog, cool!"

A bark greeted his assessment while Nala offered her hand, then pulled it back as she realized he couldn't shake. "Hello. Do you need any help with your boxes?"

"No, I'm good. I'm sure you're not coming to see me. I'd remember if I had a beautiful woman and her equally handsome dog coming to see me."

A nervous laugh greeted his remark. Blatant flirting rattled Nala since it was difficult to pinpoint if it was sincere. Extroverts could reply with clever comebacks in a second, while people like herself struggled for an appropriate reply long after the person had left. "Yeah, right."

Instead of insisting he meant it, the man grinned. "I'm Harry Chafant. I run a mail-order business on the second floor. Didn't know there were any other businesses in the building. There are some apartments in use, though. Maybe you're here to see one of the residents."

Nala shoved her hands in her jeans pockets since she didn't know what to do with them. "Ah, I'm Nala, Nala Bonne." *Oops*, she had lost a chance to try out her new name. "I'll be opening my business on the third floor. Max," she gestured to her dog, "and I are going up to check out the office."

"Really?" Harry drew out the word, and his smile grew bigger. "Today must be my lucky day. I'm headed to the post office, but when I get back I'd love to show you around."

"Thanks, but I've already seen the building." Regret stabbed her as she watched the man's smile slip. No good would come out of being too friendly to her neighbors. Even if they did hit it off, eventually they'd break up and she'd peer out her door every time a woman got buzzed in, wondering if it was her replacement. Still, she didn't want to sound unfriendly. She held up one hand. "See ya around."

"Yeah," Harry agreed and continued to descend the stairs.

If her best friend, Karly, had witnessed the scene, she'd take Nala to task, telling her she shot down another perfectly good prospect. Maybe she had, but she also avoided a messy emotional entanglement and the possibility of placing another crack in her heart. Some women threw themselves into the dating game with all the intensity of a bullfighter. A failed romance never seemed to get them down. They would just move on to the next guy. The most amazing thing about it was that there was always a next guy. In her experience, most men never passed her father's background investigation test. Oh, the joys of having a father in law enforcement.

On the third-floor landing, Nala withdrew her key to the office and opened the door. The entry office remained dusty and empty. The furniture fairies hadn't appeared overnight, not that she'd expected them to. A few words to her mother would have her scouring the design warehouse for office furniture, but she wouldn't mention it. This was something Nala wanted to accomplish on her own. With helpful, somewhat overprotective parents she seldom felt like she did much on her own. Even with school projects, she had felt they were more a group project.

Her father had built a circuit board that allowed an electrical circuit to run several items at once for the science fair. She, however, had wanted to grow plants and play music to them. When she didn't ace the science fair, her father demanded to know if the fair was fixed. It was obvious the circuit board was the superior project. Her petite teacher went toe to toe with her father and pointed out the circuit board was beyond the ability of a seven-year-old. A third-grader won with an experiment that showed tomato plants grew taller with regular shots of diet cola.

"Let's hit it." Nala dropped the leash and allowed Max to wander at will while she withdrew window cleaner, a rag, and some press-on letters. Her first project would be the exterior door.

"I'm not sure about the clear glass. If a person wants privacy they don't want everyone and their cousin peering in at them as they come to me to consult about a philandering husband or wife."

"Do people even do that anymore? I just thought they divorced, divvied up the stuff, and sometimes offloaded the family pet to a friend, relative, or took him for a ride in the country."

Nala blinked, knowing good and well no one else was in the office. She dropped her gaze to Max, who had his head cocked as if waiting for her answer. *No, it couldn't be.* Dogs didn't talk, at least not in a raspy baritone. She pinched herself just to be certain she wasn't dreaming. It hurt. *Maybe she just thought he said something. The best thing would be to test out her theory.* "Did your last owners divorce?"

Something must have happened to Max since she had picked him up at an animal shelter the day before he would have been put down. Grown dogs were only kept for a few days at the most. Then again, it could be she wanted Max to talk so she'd have someone to converse with. A fellow traveler in this new life she'd plotted out for herself.

"Nope." He grimaced, showing his teeth. "I made the mistake of talking again. Not the first time I've been ousted from a comfortable home. This last time I was driven from the house by my former owner holding a crucifix and calling me *devil dog.*"

"Weird." She shook her head hard still not convinced she wasn't dreaming. I would have thought someone would have put you on the David Letterman show. Whoops, I keep forgetting he retired." *Was she really having a conversation with her dog?*

"You'd think that." He barked a couple of times before continuing. "You gotta remember English is my third language and some things don't translate."

"You speak three languages?"

He lifted his nose with pride. "I do. Dog, of course, the silent language of scent, and I'm reasonably conversant in English. One potential owner tried to speak to me in German. Despite my muddied bloodlines, I couldn't understand a word he said. I wanted to tell him I was born in America. I didn't, since I wasn't totally sure."

"Ah, of course." She nodded her head as if she understood. *Was there anything understandable about a talking dog?* "So, when did you start talking? Are there a lot of talking dogs out there?"

His nose dropped as he stretched out and laid his head on his paws. "All dogs talk in the accepted canine dialect, except for basenjis who do this strange yodeling thing. I haven't met one who speaks English, although most do understand it very well. They might pretend not to know phrases such as stay off the couch, not for you, or not now. They do. Even though they understand English, they freak out when I say something. Something about it being us against them, meaning your kind."

"Ah." Nala searched her mind for how she had treated Max in the few days she owned him. Had she offended him somehow by treating him like a dog? "You never answered how you came to talk."

"Oh, that." He managed a few sharp yips that resembled a laugh. "Funny story. My first owner was a close-mouthed male. Not one to share his feelings or general observations about life. While this didn't bother me all that much, it was an entirely different story for his girlfriend, who happened to be a witch. She always fixed extra scrambled eggs and bacon for me when she visited, so I liked her. Anyhow, one day, she says to the man, 'If you don't talk to me, then your dog will.'"

"Just like that?"

"Took me a while to become a good conversationalist. At the time, I was so excited I voiced every thought." He lifted his head enough to display a doggy grin. "Imagine a constant litany of me listing everything I saw. Tree, grass, dog poop from the poodle two houses down, smells like she likes me. After all, she left it in front of my house. Well, you get the idea."

"Irritating."

"Yep, I discovered immediately that while people yack non-stop, they don't appreciate a talkative dog, especially my first owner who didn't even make the effort to talk to his girlfriend. One day, she was gone. Not sure if they agreed to separate. I just noticed the house smelled less like the sandalwood incense she always burned. After that, I got relocated, too."

"Where?"

"A family with kids. They had a little boy I adored. He wasn't that good at walking so he often hung onto me when he was unstable. It was only natural that I tried to encourage him. His parents were worried about his developing psyche and the dangers of believing a dog could talk. They thought I was a bad influence." Max stood, paced to the hallway and returned to his original place before circling and flopping back down on the floor.

"That's too bad about the kid. I'm not sure what I'll do with a talking dog."

A foul smell permeated the air. "Sorry." Max offered her an apologetic expression. "The Chinese food you gave me yesterday doesn't agree with me. I love it, though. Besides, stress has that effect, too."

Her intention had been to get a dog for companionship. Karly, who worked at the shelter, had emailed her pictures of dogs that would be put down. *Talk about guilt.* Even worse, when they met for lunch, she'd talk about the abandoned dogs, giving them names and listing their idiosyncrasies. Nala pointed out more than once that if Karly wanted someone to adopt a dog it was better not to mention things such as its tendency to rip up anything vaguely chewable or its midnight howling. Karly insisted people had to enter relationships with open eyes.

As if that would ever work. There was a reason woman shoved themselves into shapewear, piled on the makeup, and clipped on hair extensions. Men didn't want reality, and she was sure women didn't either. On occasion, when they needed a reality check, they'd hire an investigator. She'd specialize in date research. No woman wanted to go on a date with an online prospect or even the cousin of a co-worker and end up battered, broke or, worse, dead.

"We'll have to limit your intake to the weekends. Can't have you scaring off the clients with your toxic farts."

A hopeful gleam appeared in Max's eyes as his ears pitched forward. "Do you mean you're going to keep me?"

"Why not?"

"The talking usually scares people off, but Karly assured me you'd be okay with it. Since you're into magic, psychic skills, and all that." His long tail wagged, hitting the floor. The empty room magnified the sound.

"Karly knew? The woman who never believes in too much information withheld the fact from me that you could speak?"

"She never told you she didn't like Jeff, either."

Nala looked up from pecking at her cell with her index finger. "You mean you and Karly talked about my ex-boyfriend?"

Max swallowed hard. "You know, I could be an immense help around the detective agency."

"How so?"

"Scent. I can tell if people are lying or not by their scent."

She shook her head, imagining how well a large German shepherd mix sniffing them would go over. "I'm pretty sure my future clients and suspects wouldn't go for you sticking your nose in their crotch."

"Please." He managed a huff. "I have excellent scent ability. The nose in the crotch thing is something dogs do just for fun. It's a game we like to play with humans. If you didn't react so strongly, then it wouldn't be as hilarious."

Author Notes

The Way Over the Hill Gang series is based on spending a decade as a cook in a convalescent center. I had the opportunity to get to know the residents very well. It also explains my obsession with food in the initial story, **Late for Dinner.** There's many more great tales to follow involving the senior sleuths. The point I wanted to make is age is no barrier for getting things done. Often a mature mind has more experience to draw on as my characters demonstrate. Not all experience has to be police related either. Keep your eyes peeled for **Late for Bingo,** which is coming this fall.

Love to see you at my five annual personal appearances. In the meantime, stay in touch via my newsletter. Sign up at www.morgankwyatt.com.

Subscribers find out about exclusive freebies, contests, and personal appearances.

If you feel like writing a review, please do.

Reading takes you to your happy place.

MK Scott
www.morgankwyatt.com

Made in the USA
Monee, IL
17 May 2020

31264393R00125